GREAT LAKES
GHOST SHIP

Here's what readers from around the country are saying about Johnathan Rand's *AMERICAN CHILLERS:*

"Our whole class just finished reading 'Poisonous Pythons Paralyze Pennsylvania, and it was GREAT!"

-Trent J., age 11, Pennsylvania

"I finished reading "Dangerous Dolls of Delaware in just three days! It creeped me out!

-Brittany K., age 9, Ohio

"My teacher read GHOST IN THE GRAVEYARD to us. I loved it! I can't wait to read GHOST IN THE GRAND!"

-Nicholas H., age 8, Arizona

"My brother got in trouble for reading your book after he was supposed to go to bed. He says it's your fault, because your books are so good. But he's not mad at you or anything."

-Ariel C., age 10, South Carolina

"Thank you for coming to our school. I thought you would be scary, but you were really funny."

-Tyler D., age 10, Michigan

"American Chillers is my favorite series! Can you write them faster so I don't have to wait for the next one? Thank you."

-Alex W., age 8, Washington, D.C.

"I can't stop reading AMERICAN CHILLERS! I've read every one twice, and I'm going to read them again!"

-Emilee T., age 12, Wisconsin

"Our whole class listened to CREEPY CAMPFIRE CHILLERS with the lights out. It was really spooky!"

-*Erin J., age 12, Georgia*

"When you write a book about Oklahoma, write it about my city. I've lived here all my life, and it's a freaky place."

-*Justin P., age 11, Oklahoma*

"When you came to our school, you said that all of your books are true stories. I don't believe you, but I LOVE your books, anyway!"

-*Anthony H., age 11, Ohio*

"I really liked NEW YORK NINJAS! I'm going to get all of your books!"

-*Chandler L., age 10, New York*

"Every night I read your books in bed with a flashlight. You write really creepy stories!"

-*Skylar P., age 8, Michigan*

"My teacher let me borrow INVISIBLE IGUANAS OF ILLINOIS, and I just finished it! It was really, really great!"

-*Greg R., age 11, Virginia*

"I went to your website and saw your dogs. They are really cute. Why don't you write a book about them?"

-*Laura L., age 10, Arkansas*

"DANGEROUS DOLLS OF DELAWARE was so scary that I couldn't read it at night. Then I had a bad dream. That book was super-freaky!"

-*Sean F., age 9, Delaware*

"I have every single book in the CHILLERS series, and I love them!"

-*Mike W., age 11, Michigan*

"Your books rock!"

-*Darrell D ., age 10, Minnesota*

"My friend let me borrow one of your books, and now I can't stop! So far, my favorite is WISCONSIN WEREWOLVES. That was a great book!"

-*Riley S., age 12, Oregon*

"I read your books every single day. They're COOL!"

-*Katie M., age 12, Michigan*

"I just found out that the #14 book is called CREEPY CONDORS OF CALIFORNIA. That's where I live! I can't wait for this book!"

-*Emilio H., age 10, California*

"I have every single book that you've written, and I can't decide which one I love the most! Keep writing!"

-*Jenna S., age 9, Kentucky*

"I love to read your books! My brother does, too!"

-*Joey B., age 12, Missouri*

"I got IRON INSECTS INVADE INDIANA for my birthday, and it's AWESOME!"

-*Colin T., age 10, Indiana*

Don't miss these exciting, action-packed books by Johnathan Rand:

Michigan Chillers:

#1: Mayhem on Mackinac Island
#2: Terror Stalks Traverse City
#3: Poltergeists of Petoskey
#4: Aliens Attack Alpena
#5: Gargoyles of Gaylord
#6: Strange Spirits of St. Ignace
#7: Kreepy Klowns of Kalamazoo
#8: Dinosaurs Destroy Detroit
#9: Sinister Spiders of Saginaw
#10: Mackinaw City Mummies
#11: Great Lakes Ghost Ship
#12: AuSable Alligators
#13: Gruesome Ghouls of Grand Rapids
#14: Bionic Bats of Bay City

American Chillers:

#1: The Michigan Mega-Monsters
#2: Ogres of Ohio
#3: Florida Fog Phantoms
#4: New York Ninjas
#5: Terrible Tractors of Texas
#6: Invisible Iguanas of Illinois
#7: Wisconsin Werewolves
#8: Minnesota Mall Mannequins
#9: Iron Insects Invade Indiana
#10: Missouri Madhouse
#11: Poisonous Pythons Paralyze Pennsylvania
#12: Dangerous Dolls of Delaware
#13: Virtual Vampires of Vermont
#14: Creepy Condors of California
#15: Nebraska Nightcrawlers
#16: Alien Androids Assault Arizona
#17: South Carolina Sea Creatures
#18: Washington Wax Museum
#19: North Dakota Night Dragons

Adventure Club series:

#1: Ghost in the Graveyard
#2: Ghost in the Grand
#3: The Haunted Schoolhouse

Freddie Fernortner, Fearless First Grader:

#1: The Fantastic Flying Bicycle
#2: The Super-Scary Night Thingy
#3: A Haunting We Will Go
#4: Freddie's Dog Walking Service
#5: The Big Box Fort
#6: Mr. Chewy's Big Adventure
#7: The Magical Wading Pool

#11: Great Lakes Ghost Ship

An AudioCraft Publishing, Inc. book

This book is a work of fiction. Names, places, characters and incidents are used fictitiously, or are products of the author's very active imagination.

Book storage and warehouses provided by Chillermania!©
Indian River, Michigan

Warehouse security provided by:
Lily Munster and Scooby-Boo

Michigan Chillers #11: Great Lakes Ghost Ship
ISBN 13-digit: 978-1-893699-84-7

Librarians/Media Specialists:
PCIP/MARC records available at www.americanchillers.com

Cover illustration by Dwayne Harris
Cover layout and design by Sue Harring

Printed in USA

GREAT LAKES
GHOST SHIP

VISIT CHILLERMANIA!

WORLD HEADQUARTERS FOR BOOKS BY JOHNATHAN RAND!

Yooperland

Indian River

Alpena

Traverse City

MICHIGAN

CHILLERMANIA!

*I-75 Exit 313
then south
1 mile!*

Mt. Pleasant

Bay City

Grand Rapids

Lansing

Detroit

Kalamazoo

Visit the HOME for books by Johnathan Rand! Featuring books, hats, shirts, bookmarks and other cool stuff not available anywhere else in the world! Plus, watch the American Chillers website for news of special events and signings at *CHILLERMANIA!* with author Johnathan Rand! Located in northern lower Michigan, on I-75! Take exit 313 . . . then south 1 mile! For more info, call (231) 238-0338. And be afraid! Be veeeery afraaaaaaiiiid . . . .

On a particular day in October, my family traveled from our home in Grand Blanc, Michigan, to Cheboygan. Cheboygan is a small town in northern lower Michigan, not far from the Mackinac Bridge.

I remember the day so well because something really weird happened. When we left Grand Blanc, it was raining. However, by the time we arrived in Cheboygan, the rain had stopped. The sun was setting, and the air was actually kind of warm—for October, anyway. October is when the temperatures start to get pretty chilly in our state.

But that wasn't the weird part.

The weird part was that as soon as I got out of the car, I got this really creepy feeling, like something just wasn't right. I didn't know what it was. My brother, Brian, felt it, too.

After we unpacked and went inside to say hello to Grandma and Grandpa, Brian and I walked back outside.

"Did you feel that, Emilee?" my brother asked. "When we first got here? Did you get a real creepy feeling?"

"Yeah," I said, glancing up and down the street. "It felt like all of the hair on my head was going to stand on end."

We stood in the final rays of daylight, looking around. Our grandparents live just outside of town in a quiet neighborhood. Other houses lined the street, and big trees with spiny, bare branches reached up into the sky. Most of the leaves had already turned brown and fallen off, but there were a few stubborn ones that remained. The air was heavy and damp. It was still kind of warm, but I knew that the coming night would bring colder temperatures.

"Maybe we just imagined it," I said.

"Maybe," Brian agreed. He looked around. "Come on. Let's see if we can find Gavin before it gets dark."

We met Gavin Stewart a long time ago, when I was only four or five years old. He lives in Cheboygan, and whenever we visit our grandparents, we always go to his house, which is only a few blocks away. Although we only see him a few times a year, he's a really good friend. He's eleven—which is how old I am. Brian is a year younger.

We walked down the street toward his house. When we got there, his home was dark, and there were no cars in the driveway. It was obvious that the Stewart family was gone.

But there was more to it than that.

"Well, maybe we'll see him tomorrow," I said, looking at the dark house. "Tomorrow is Saturday, and we'll have all day to hang out."

Suddenly, that same creepy feeling—the one I'd felt when we'd first arrived—fell over me.

I looked around, and that's when I noticed something odd.

"Brian . . . look," I said quietly, pointing at other houses along the same side of the street.

"What is it?" he replied, his voice barely a whisper.

"None of the lights are on in any of these houses," I said. "On the other side of the street, there are lights on. It's getting dark fast . . . but nobody has their lights on over on this side."

"That's weird," Brian said. He scratched his head.

I looked at the row of dark houses.

So did Brian.

And when I looked into an empty, dark window, that's when I saw it.

A ghost.

I gasped, and I think I jumped a foot into the air. Brian saw the ghost at the same time I did. He shrieked and covered his mouth with his hands.

In the window was the ghostly figure of a man. He was staring back at us in the dim evening. His face was expressionless.

I wanted to run, but my legs felt all rubbery. Brian grabbed my arm so hard that it hurt.

Suddenly, the ghost opened the window. "Is everything all right?" he asked.

I breathed a sigh. It wasn't a ghost, after all. It was just a man. From behind the dark window, he only *looked* like a ghost.

"We thought you were a ghost," I said sheepishly. "I guess we were scared for a minute."

The man laughed. "No ghosts here," he said, looking around the yard. "Not yet, anyway." Then he laughed again, but it was a nervous laugh.

"How come there are no lights on this side of the street?" Brian asked.

"Power failure," the man replied. He pointed toward the end of the block. "We had a storm earlier today, and a tree fell on the power lines a few blocks away. The power is supposed to be back on in a little while."

That made sense. We had the same thing happen to us last summer at our home in Grand Blanc.

"We were looking for our friend, Gavin Stewart," Brian said, pointing to the house next door.

"The Stewarts went to Traverse City," the man replied. "I think they'll be back later tonight."

Cool!

"Thanks," I said to the man. He nodded and closed the window.

The sun had set, but there was an amber-colored glow in the western sky. The air was getting chillier fast.

"Come on, Brian," I said. "Let's go home."

We started walking back toward our grandparents' house.

"I'm glad that Grandma and Grandpa still have electricity," I said. "That would be a bummer to have driven all the way up here, only to find out that they had no power."

Brian didn't say anything, and we walked along in silence. Our sneakers whispered on the concrete sidewalk. There were no other sounds, except for the hum of a few cars several blocks away.

Suddenly, Brian stopped.

"What do you think that man meant, Emilee?" he asked.

I stopped, turned around, and looked at him. "What do you mean?" I replied.

"I mean . . . did you hear what he said when you told him that we thought he was a ghost?"

"Yeah," I said. "He said that there were no ghosts around here."

"Yeah, but did you see what he did next?" Brian asked. "He looked around and then said 'not yet, anyway'. And he looked kind of nervous. What do you suppose he meant by that?"

I guess I hadn't thought about it. But the more I recalled what the man had said, the stranger his behavior seemed. The man had looked around, like he actually *might* see a ghost.

Not yet, anyway.

That's exactly what he had said.

Not yet, anyway.

What did he mean by that?

We would find out, all right . . . a lot sooner than we had expected.

3

By the next morning, the rain had started again. Brian and I ate breakfast with Mom, Dad, Grandpa, and Grandma. We talked and laughed a lot. Grandpa and Grandma wanted to know how school was going for us, how my Girl Scout troop was doing, and what we'd been up to.

After breakfast, we went for a long car ride. We saw a few deer, and a red fox near the side of the road. We drove all the way to Mackinaw City, where we ate lunch. Then, we drove home.

It was mid-afternoon by the time we returned to Cheboygan. The rain was still falling on and off, so Brian and I borrowed an umbrella and went outside, heading for Gavin's house. The air was cool and damp. Puddles of water pooled in the yard and in the road, and rain thrummed on the umbrella. The bare trees were black and shiny, and rain dripped from their branches.

"I hope it doesn't rain all weekend," I said, as we walked along the wet sidewalk.

"Me, too," Brian said. "If it stops, we can go to the park and the marina."

We arrived at Gavin's house and knocked on the door. His mom answered.

"Why, hello, Emilee! Hello, Brian!" she exclaimed, opening the door wider. "Come in! Gavin will be so happy to see you!"

We stepped inside.

"Gavin!" Mrs. Stewart called out. "Brian and Emilee Beech are here!"

We heard a shuffling noise upstairs. Then footsteps pounded the stairs. Gavin came through the kitchen and into the living room.

"Hey, guys!" he exclaimed. His blue eyes were wide, and his blond hair was longer than I remembered. "I didn't know you were coming up this weekend!"

"We didn't, either," I said. "Our grandparents invited us to come, and Dad had the weekend off. We drove up from Grand Blanc yesterday."

We talked for a while, and he told us about some of the fun things he'd done since we'd seen each other last. I told him about the science project we did at school that almost started a fire.

It was still raining outside, so we played checkers for a while. Then, we took turns playing a video game.

After an hour or so, the rain finally quit, which was a good thing, because we were all tired of being cooped up inside.

"Let's walk down to Gordon Turner Park," Gavin suggested. "We can stop at the store on the way and get a candy bar or something."

"That sounds cool," I said. Gordon Turner Park is near the mouth of the Cheboygan River, where it flows into Lake Huron. It's a pretty popular park.

I left the umbrella on Gavin's porch, and the three of us hopscotched around puddles in the driveway. When we reached the sidewalk, we turned and headed toward town.

"Hey, there's where the tree fell on the power line," I said, after we'd walked several blocks.

We stopped and stared. Actually, it wasn't a tree that had fallen, but a huge branch. A strong wind must have snapped it off, and it had fallen on the power lines. It was in pieces on the wet grass. There were several small piles of sawdust where the giant limb had been cut.

"Looks like it's all fixed now," Brian said.

"They had it fixed last night," Gavin said. "When we got back from Traverse City, the power was still off. But it came back on a few minutes after we got home."

Then I remembered the man we'd seen in the house next to Gavin's, and how we'd thought he was a ghost.

But I also remembered what he'd said.

Not yet, anyway.

No ghosts around.

Not yet, anyway.

I decided to ask Gavin about it.

"You know," I began, "the man that lives next to you said something kind of strange." I explained how we thought that we'd seen a ghost, because there were no lights on in his house, and we could only see shadows. I also explained how he had looked around the yard and said that there weren't any ghosts around . . . *not yet, anyway.*

"What did he mean by that?" I asked.

Gavin stopped walking and looked at me.

Then he looked at Brian.

Then he looked away.

"Well, it *is* October," Gavin said quietly. "Some people believe that it's true."

"Believe *what* is true?" Brian asked.

"The legend about the Great Lakes Ghost Ship," Brian said. "Of course, it's only a legend. It's not really true."

As soon as he said those words, a cool breeze caused the bare tree limbs to shudder. Several leaves, brown and brittle, fell around us like large paper snowflakes.

And, yet again, that strange, spooky feeling fell over me.

But when Gavin explained the legend of the Great Lakes Ghost Ship to us, I realized that I had good reason to be spooked.

And soon, I would be more than spooked.

I would be more than just scared.

I would be terrified . . . as Brian, Gavin, and I were about to have the most horrifying experience of our lives.

Here's what Gavin told us:

The US Coast Guard Cutter *Mackinaw* is stationed in Cheboygan. The boat is big: two hundred ninety feet long and seventy-five feet wide. It has a crew of about ninety men and women, and the boat is used to break ice and keep the shipping lanes on the Great Lakes open during the cold winter months. There are other things that the cutter is used for, like emergency rescues and things like that. But mostly, it's used to break ice to allow big freighters and other ships to navigate the waters.

Well, there is a legend that every October, an old sea captain sometimes appears around Cheboygan, inviting people to come aboard his ship. He walks the streets at night, and can appear anywhere. If you follow him, he'll take you aboard the cutter *Mackinaw* . . . which turns into a ghost ship.

"They say the ghost ship is really creepy," Gavin said, "with all kinds of strange zombie sailors wandering around on board. My uncle is stationed aboard the cutter, and he says that some of the crew members have seen some of the zombies."

"Wow," Brian gasped.

"Of course," Gavin continued, "that's just a legend. It's not really true. Some people believe it, though."

"What about you?" Brian asked. "Do you believe it?"

Gavin shook his head. "Naw," he said. "There's no such thing. Someone just made that story up."

"Where is the Coast Guard cutter?" I asked.

"It's moored at the mouth of the Cheboygan River," Gavin answered. He pointed. "Over that way. It's not far from the park."

"Could we go see it?" Brian asked.

Gavin shrugged. "I guess so. My uncle gave me a tour once. It's pretty cool inside. I mean . . . it's a lot bigger than you think. It's like walking through a big apartment building, up and down stairs and everything."

"That sounds cool," I said. I've only seen smaller boats, and a big ship like the *Mackinaw* sounded like it would be fun to see.

We turned down the next block, crossed a main street, and headed down a long drive. At the end of the drive, we turned left.

Suddenly, there it was.

The *Mackinaw*.

It was mostly red, with big white lettering on the side.

nd, like Gavin said, it was *huge!* I had never seen a ship so big in my life.

Not this close, anyway.

"Can we get closer?" Brian asked.

"Yeah," Gavin said. "But we won't be allowed to go on board."

"That's okay," I said. "I think it'll be cool just getting a better look at it."

We walked through a large, gravel parking lot. Pebbles crunched beneath our feet. With every step, the enormous red vessel loomed larger and larger.

Finally, we stopped. We were only about thirty feet from the massive cutter.

"Wow," Brian breathed. "This thing is super-gargantuan!"

We didn't see anybody on board, but Gavin explained that most of the time the crew stayed within the ship.

Suddenly, one of the doors on the ship opened up, and a man wearing a blue uniform stepped out.

"Gavin? Is that you?"

"Uncle Pete!" Gavin exclaimed. He waved his hand.

"I thought that was you," Gavin's uncle replied. "I saw you and your friends through the window."

"This is Emilee and Brian," Gavin said. "They're my friends from Grand Blanc. They're here for the weekend."

"That's super," Gavin's uncle said. "I've got a few minutes. Maybe you and your friends would like to tour the ship."

I couldn't believe what I was hearing! Not only did we get to see the outside of the ship . . . but now, we had the chance to go inside and look around!

"Yeah!" Gavin said. "That would be great!"

"Come aboard," Gavin's uncle said, motioning with his arm. We raced to the edge of the dock and carefully followed the narrow metal gangplank onto the boat.

This is so cool! I thought. *Wait until I tell my friends back home about this!*

Well, I would have more to tell my friends than I could have ever imagined. I would be able to tell them not only about the tour . . . but about all of the horrifying things that were about to happen.

5

The inside of the *Mackinaw* was incredible. We went down steep stairs, climbed ladders, and descended into the depths of the ship. Sometimes the rooms were cozy and big, but other places were cold and dark and gray. The smell of diesel fumes was really strong in some places, but not so much so in others. Cables and wires ran along the ceilings and stretched down walls.

And it was noisy! There were all kinds of sounds: rumblings, gratings, electrical sounds, drumming sounds . . . all different kinds of sounds.

"And it's ten times louder when the ship sets sail," Gavin's uncle explained. "When the big engines are fired up, you can hear them all through the ship."

It was really a fascinating experience, and I realized that if you didn't know where you were going, you could very easily get lost.

We didn't see any other crew members, which I thought was strange.

"Where is everybody?" I asked.

"Today is a busy day for everyone," Gavin's uncle explained. "There are lots of things going on, and most of the crew are in last-minute preparations. I'm pretty busy, too, but I've got a few minutes to—"

He was interrupted by a sharp, shrill ringing sound that came from a pager clipped to his belt. He unsnapped it and looked at it closely.

"I've got to run to the bridge for a moment," he said. Then he replaced his pager and looked at us. "I'll need you three to stay right here. Don't go anywhere until I come back. Understand?"

We all nodded. Gavin's uncle spun and vanished up a ladder that led into the ceiling. In seconds he was gone, and I was amazed at how fast he could maneuver around the ship in such tight places.

"This is so cool!" Brian said to Gavin. "I never thought I'd ever get a chance to be on a ship like this!"

"Yeah," I said. "Thanks, Gavin!"

"Don't thank me," he said. "I didn't even think we'd see my uncle. You can thank him when he comes back."

But Gavin's Uncle Pete didn't come back.

We waited.

And we waited some more.

And we waited even more, listening to the sounds of the ship all around us. We talked for a few minutes, but when Gavin's uncle still hadn't returned, we grew silent.

Once again, I had that nervous, odd feeling creep through my body.

Something's not right, I thought. *Gavin's uncle should have been back by now.*

And another thing that bothered me:

I kept thinking about the legend of the Great Lakes Ghost Ship. Sure, I knew it was only a legend, and the story of the old sea captain was only make-believe. There wasn't *really* a ghost ship, and there were no monsters inside of it.

But still—

Finally, I heard footsteps on metal. Gavin's uncle was coming back.

"Sheesh," Gavin said. "It's about time. He's been gone for half an hour!"

A door opened, but what came through it wasn't Gavin's uncle.

It wasn't even another Coast Guard officer.

I gasped.

Brian drew a breath and made a choking sound.

Gavin didn't say anything, but I knew that he was just as freaked out as I was.

What came through the door was the most hideous, ugly creature I had ever seen.

A zombie sailor.

And that's when I realized that the legend of the Great Lakes Ghost Ship wasn't just a legend.

It was real.

Not only was it real . . . but we were on board.

We were on board . . . and if the legend was true—

We might be here forever!

If I had to describe the creature, I would say he looked just like Gavin had said: like a zombie. He was dressed like a sailor, but his clothing was tattered. And he had a human face—sort of. His skin was pasty-white, and there was no doubt that he wasn't alive. How he moved around, I don't know—but a creature that repulsive couldn't possibly live and breathe and have a heartbeat. His hair was all messy and nasty looking, and I wondered if, perhaps, the thing wasn't real at all.

Maybe he was a ghost.

But the good thing was, he hadn't spotted us.

Yet.

We had to hide, and fast. I think that Brian and Gavin had the same idea.

Quickly, and without speaking, we sank back behind several large, fifty-gallon drums, and tucked down against the wall. It was a tight fit, and the three of us were squished together, but we did it.

Meanwhile, we could hear the horrible, zombie-like creature coming closer and closer, and the only thing we could do was hope that he wouldn't see us.

A shadow fell across the barrels. We could actually hear the creature—whatever he was—breathing as he walked past.

He breathed out. *Hooooooooooooooo.*

He breathed in. *Heeeeeeeeeeeeeee.*

In. *Hooooooooooooooo* . . .

Out. *Heeeeeeeeeeeeeee* . . .

Whatever he was, he was only a few feet away.

Hooooooooooooooo . . .

Heeeeeeeeeeeeeee . . .

Suddenly, he walked right in front of us! I could have reached out and touched him if I wanted to.

But I wouldn't have done that in a million years!

The three of us waited, holding our breaths, hoping that the hideous zombie wouldn't see us, that he would just simply pass by and go somewhere—anywhere—as long as he went away.

Finally, we couldn't see the zombie sailor anymore.

There were no more footsteps.

No more sounds, except the sounds of the ship all around us.

"Do . . . do you think he's gone?" Brian whispered.

"I don't know," Gavin replied. *"I just hope that Uncle Pete comes back quick."*

"What if he doesn't?" I asked.

"He will," Gavin said, but he didn't sound very convinced himself.

"Was . . . was that . . . one of those . . . those zombie sailors you were telling us about?" I stammered. *"From the legend?"*

"I never believed that the legend was true," Gavin whispered. *"I mean . . . I didn't think it was."*

We were silent, listening to the sounds of the ship. The more time went by, the more we realized that, maybe, Gavin's uncle wasn't coming back.

He couldn't have forgotten about us, could he? Or maybe something happened to him.

Maybe . . .

Maybe he turned into a zombie.

No, Emilee, I thought. *That's crazy. That's not possible.*

But, then again, that zombie-thingy wasn't possible, either . . . and yet we saw him with our own eyes.

"We've got to find a way off the ship," Gavin finally whispered. *"Something must have happened to Uncle Pete."*

"But which way do we go?" Brian asked. *"I have no idea where we are."*

40

"It can't be that difficult to find our way off the ship," Gavin said. *"How big can the ship be?"*

The size of the ship, however, wasn't our biggest problem.

Our problem was the fact that we were about to find out that we were no longer on the Coast Guard cutter.

I know it sounds impossible . . . but it was true.

The Coast Guard cutter was no longer.

The cutter *Mackinaw* was gone, and we were prisoners . . . on the Great Lakes Ghost Ship.

We waited for a few more minutes, just listening and watching. We saw no one, and didn't hear anything besides the normal sounds of the ship.

Gavin was the first to crawl out from behind the barrels where we were hiding.

"Let's go," he said. "Let's get out of here."

We really didn't have any other option. If we stayed hidden, that zombie sailor probably wouldn't find us—but we wouldn't be any closer to leaving the ship.

Brian stood up, and I followed. It had been sort of cramped where we'd been hiding, so I stretched for a minute. Brian did, too.

And I must say, I was more than just a little freaked out. While I found the legend of the Great Lakes Ghost Ship hard to believe, I knew what I had seen. Brian and Gavin saw him, too.

A zombie sailor.

Gavin headed down the narrow passageway. There were stairs leading down, deeper into the ship, and we passed them. I didn't know where they led to, but I was certain that we didn't want to go lower. Somehow, we had to go up, higher, to another level. Or maybe two. I wasn't sure just how deep in the ship we were.

"Let's go up there," Gavin said, pointing. Ahead of us was a ladder of sorts, built into the wall. The rungs were made of metal, and fastened to the wall. They lead up through a small porthole in the ceiling.

"What's up there?" Brian asked.

"Beats me," Gavin replied with a shrug. "But we've got to go up to the main deck. This might go up there."

Gavin grabbed the ladder and quickly scrambled up. When his head reached the portal, he slowly peeked up and looked around suspiciously. Then he glanced down at us.

"All clear," he said. Then he scrambled up through the porthole and vanished.

"Go," I said to Brian, and my brother grasped a rung, placed his foot on a lower rung, and pulled himself up. He's always been good at climbing, and he ascended the ladder like a monkey. In seconds, he, too, was through the porthole.

I grabbed a rung and pulled myself up. Like Brian, I can climb pretty well, too, and I didn't have any difficulty climbing the ladder and pulling myself up through the hole.

But just as I turned and was about to stand, my shoe caught on a piece of steel. When I tried to pull it away, my shoe peeled off my foot. Before I could do anything, it had fallen . . . bouncing off one of the steel ladder rungs and tumbling to the floor below.

"Darn," I hissed, looking down through the porthole. My shoe was on the floor at the bottom of the ladder.

"What happened?" Gavin asked. He hadn't seen my shoe fall.

"I lost my shoe," I said, still staring at the white sneaker on the floor some eight feet below. "I've got to go get it."

"Hurry up," Brian said, looking around nervously. "I want to get out of here."

I grabbed a rung and descended down the ladder. When I reached the floor, I grabbed my shoe, untied the laces, slipped it onto my foot, and retied it. Then I grasped a rung, and was about to climb back up—

And that's when I heard a noise from behind me.

A shuffling of feet.

I turned slowly, looking over my shoulder. I was hoping that it would be Gavin's uncle, coming to get us.

At least, that's what I was *hoping*.

But something told me I was wrong. Something told me that Gavin's uncle wasn't coming back, that he wasn't coming to find us and lead us off the ship.

I saw a movement, and I realized that I was right.

It wasn't Gavin's uncle.

It was another zombie sailor.

Just like the one we'd seen a few minutes ago.

There was just one *big* difference: the zombie we'd seen a few minutes ago hadn't seen us.

This zombie, I was sure, had spotted me. I know this because he stopped suddenly, staring back at me with his cold, dead eyes.

He was looking at me.

I was looking at him.

He studied me curiously, like I was some kind of strange animal. In truth, *he* was the strange one.

Then, he smiled a horrible, *horrible* smile. His teeth were blackened. Some were missing.

And that's when he started toward me . . . .

I didn't even take time to *think*.

Instinctively, I pulled myself up the ladder faster than I have ever climbed anything in my life. I scrambled through the hole and jumped to my feet.

"One of those things is down there!" I shrieked.

That was all I needed to say. Gavin and Brian knew what I meant, and the three of us took off running.

Problem was, we were still just as lost as ever, and we had no idea where we were going.

But we knew where we didn't want to be: anywhere near a crazed, zombie sailor.

We ran through open doorways, which weren't like any doorways I'd ever seen before. Most doors are rectangular, but many of these were rounded and oblong-shaped. At the time, however, I didn't pay too much attention to them. I was too worried about that freaky zombie coming after us.

Ahead, we saw a rack of suits. I learned later that they were 'dry suits' used by divers for scuba diving. There were a bunch of them hanging on thick hangers near a wall.

"Over there!" I said. "We can hide behind those things!"

Brian and Gavin didn't argue. We darted quickly through the rubbery suits, snuggling as far as we could within. I wasn't even sure if the zombie was after us or not, but I wasn't going to take any chances.

And I was glad we *did* hide.

Just a few seconds later, the zombie appeared, and there was no doubt that he was looking for us. As I peered around the suits, I could see him walking slowly, cautiously, glancing from side to side. And he was having difficulty walking, too, like he had a limp or something. He was dressed a lot like the first one we'd seen, only this one had a deep scar on his cheek. His face was pasty-white, and his eyes had dark circles around them.

Behind me, snuggled within the dry suits, I heard my brother gulp. Thankfully, it wasn't loud enough for the zombie to hear. But I knew that Brian had seen the zombie, and he was totally freaked out.

And I couldn't blame him. I was totally freaked out, too.

The zombie continued on his way, and, once again, we waited in silence, just listening to the sounds of the ship, happy that the creature hadn't spotted us.

"*What else do you know about this 'Ghost Ship'?*" I asked Gavin quietly, after I was certain that the zombie was gone.

Gavin shook his head. "*Not much,*" he whispered back. "*I didn't even believe the legend.*"

"*What about now?*" Brian asked, his voice shaking. "*Now what do you believe?*"

"*I believe . . . I believe we've got to find a way off this ship,*" Gavin replied. "*We've got to get out of here, and then we'll figure things out.*"

"*Yeah, then we'll call the police!*" Brian whispered.

"*Yeah, right,*" I whispered back, rolling my eyes. "*What are we going to tell them to do? Arrest the zombies?*"

We waited, listening and watching for any more zombie sailors. When none came, we cautiously emerged from our hiding places within the hanging dry suits.

And, once again, we still had no idea how to get off the ship.

If we even *could* get off the ship.

"I think we have to go up one more level," Gavin said thoughtfully. "I'm not sure, but I think we're just beneath the main deck. If we can find our way up to the next level, we might be able to get out of here."

"But what about the legend?" Brian asked. "You said that whoever goes aboard the ghost ship gets stuck there forever."

"I don't know," Gavin said. "But we've got to try and get out of here. We've *got* to."

Slowly, we made our way down a hall lined with big iron pipes. Thick cables snaked above us. We came to yet another set of stairs that descended lower into the ship. There was a lot of noise coming from below, and I figured that we must be close to the engine room.

"Up ahead!" Brian suddenly exclaimed. "There are steps leading up!"

Sure enough, there was a steep stairway that rose up through a small opening. If Gavin was right, we would emerge on the main deck . . . and we might be able to leave the ship.

If we were lucky.

We ran to the stairs. Gavin darted up first. I followed, and Brian came up right behind me.

And when we emerged on the next level, Gavin was staring and pointing.

"Look at that!" he exclaimed. "Look!"

Gavin was pointing to a window.

I know that it might not be a big deal to *you,* but to us, it was huge.

It was a window to the outside!

It was getting dark, but we could see gray, overcast clouds. It was the greatest feeling in the world. I couldn't believe it. Seeing a window in the ship was like a window to the world.

A window . . . *home.*

We raced to it, pressing our noses against the cool glass and peering outside. Unfortunately, the window wasn't dockside . . . meaning that all we saw was the water and some houses and trees on the other side of the river. I was hoping that maybe we would be able to wave for help, but there was no one else around. Even if there were, they would be on the other side of the river, and they probably wouldn't be able to see us, anyway.

So, once again, we were stuck.

"Doesn't the window open?" Brian asked.

Gavin shook his head. "Not this one," he said. "This one looks like it's made to stay right where it is. My uncle said that some of the windows don't open, because they have to be strong enough for the worst of storms."

"So, we're no better off now than we were before," I said.

"Not really," Gavin replied hopefully. "At least we're on the main deck. All we have to do is make it to the other side of this ship. That shouldn't be too hard."

I wish he wouldn't have said that.

Because maybe if he *hadn't* said it, it *might* have been easy. We *might* have made it to the other side of the ship.

As it turned out, our troubles were only beginning . . . starting when we heard a rattling of chains from above . . . .

The sounds sent a thunderstorm of shivers through my body. The rattling of chains—thick and heavy—seemed to worm right into my bones.

We looked up at the maze of steel pipes and wires that mapped the ceiling.

"What in the world is that noise?" Brian whispered.

"It sounds like chains," Gavin replied.

"Is this what happens when it turns into the ghost ship?" I asked.

Gavin shrugged. "I don't know," he replied. "Like I said before: I didn't think that the legend was true."

The chains kept rattling. It was the spookiest sound I think I have ever heard in my life.

"Well, it's not doing us any good to stay here," Gavin said. "Let's keep looking for a way out."

"Let's try and stay away from those zombies," Brian said. "One of those things could really mess up my day."

We followed a narrow passageway, nervously looking all around as we walked, hoping that we wouldn't encounter another one of those creepy sailors. The rattling of chains faded as we walked, and soon, all we could hear was the normal humming sounds of the ship.

It wasn't long, however, before we heard more footsteps coming toward us.

We stopped suddenly, trying to figure out where the sounds were coming from.

One thing was certain: it sounded like two or three people walking.

As much as we hoped that the footsteps would be from the Coast Guard crew, we couldn't take any chances. We had to hide, and fast.

Gavin turned his head to the left, then snapped it around to the right. He pointed.

There was a thin hallway that extended off to the right. At the very end was a big footlocker—big enough for all three of us to hide in—if it was open.

We raced to it. Thankfully, not only was the locker open, but it was almost empty. There were only a couple of life vests inside.

"Hurry!" Gavin whispered frantically. *"Inside!"*

We climbed into the footlocker. The sound of footsteps drew nearer, louder. We huddled into the locker, and Gavin pulled the lid down. From inside, we could leave the lid open a tiny crack and see out.

And I'll tell you this: I'm glad we hid when we did. Not two seconds after we had scrambled into the footlocker, a zombie appeared. He was walking backwards, moving clumsily and slowly. He was carrying something.

Something *big*.

The zombie was carrying one end of a long, dark box. As he passed by, another zombie appeared. He, too, was walking slowly, struggling with the big box.

Only then did we realize what the zombies were carrying.

Not a box.

Not a crate.

A coffin . . . .

If I hadn't been scared enough, the sight of the two zombies carrying the coffin made me want to scream.

But I couldn't. If I did, the creatures would hear me, and they would come after us. I was sure of that.

Gavin lowered the lid, and the thin bar of light vanished. We were in complete darkness, cramped and huddled together.

And somehow, that made me feel a little better. Oh, I was still freaked out, but knowing that we were in the footlocker where we couldn't be seen made me feel a little safer.

At least for the time being.

"What are those things carrying a coffin for?" Brian asked quietly.

"I don't have any idea," Gavin whispered back. "This is all new to me, too."

"Well, we can't stay in this thing," I said. "What if one of them finds us here?"

"Hey, at least we're hidden," Brian said. "I say we just wait here until someone comes to find us."

"Who's going to come and find us?" I asked. "Nobody knows where we are."

"Yeah," Gavin said. "I told my mom that we were going to Gordon Turner Park. If anybody is looking for us, they'll have no idea that we're on the Coast Guard cutter."

"Your uncle knows," Brian said.

"Yeah," Gavin agreed, "but we don't know where he is or what's happened to him. For all we know, those creatures might have got him."

"He might even be a zombie sailor himself," Brian said.

The more and more we thought about it, the more we realized that we would just have to continue on through the ship, dodging zombies, until we found a way out.

If there *was* a way out. At the moment, our chances didn't look very good.

"Well, we know that we need to get to the opposite side of the ship," Gavin said. "There seems to be more zombies up at this level than there are below. Maybe we could go back down into the ship and make our way to the other side. Then we could find our way back up to the main deck."

The plan sounded risky, but we really didn't have any other options. And besides—Gavin was right. If there were more zombies up here, near the main deck, we might be able to get away from them and stay out of sight on the lower decks. There were a lot more places to hide down there, too.

Gavin raised the lid of the footlocker, and a thin band of light filtered in. The hallway was empty, and we didn't hear any footsteps.

"Let's go," he whispered, pushing the lid open farther.

In seconds, we had scrambled out of the locker and were at the intersection of the halls. We saw no one.

Whew.

"Over there," Brian said, pointing toward a ladder that vanished within a hole in the floor.

Quietly and quickly, we walked to it and peered down. Gavin got on his hands and knees and poked his head through the hole.

"All clear," he said, and he grasped a steel rung and descended the ladder. I was next, and Brian followed. When we reached the floor, we found yet another stairway that led even farther down into the ship. The humming sounds grew louder, and I figured that we must be somewhere near the engine room.

Gavin wasted no time descending the steep stairs. Again, I followed, with Brian right on my heels.

Sure enough, we were back at the engine room. Although the motors weren't on, the noise sure was loud. I figured that there must be some other smaller motors running to power other things on the ship.

And so far, we hadn't seen any more zombies. Gavin was right: for whatever reason, there seemed to be less of them down here than there were on the upper decks. If we could just make it to the other side of the ship, I was sure we would find a way out.

Problem was, the cutter was a big, big ship—and getting to the other side was going to be a lot harder than we thought.

You see, there was one thing that we hadn't thought about.

Something awful.

And it was about to happen.

In the engine room, the air was heavy with the thick smell of grease and diesel fumes.

And the engines were gigantic! Each one was the size of a truck! I had never seen engines so big in my life.

The floor beneath us was interesting, too. It wasn't really a floor, but a metal grate. I could see another level beneath the engine room. It was kind of weird, walking on a grate, looking down into yet another room.

To the left and right, there were some workbenches against the wall too. I think what I found most surprising is how clean it was. Dad likes to work on his car, and he has tools scattered all over our garage. There are grease and oil stains on the floor and on his workbench. Here, however, in the engine room of the *Mackinaw,* the area was spotless.

We made our way over the grate and around the big engines. There were several short flights of stairs we had to climb, but soon, we were on the other side of the room.

But now we had a problem.

Oh, there weren't any zombies around, which was a good thing.

But the rattling of chains began again . . . along with other sounds.

Ghostly sounds, like loud creaking.

And *moans.*

It was faint, but we could definitely hear the sound of people moaning and groaning, and terrible shrieks and wicked laughter.

"What in the world is that?" I whispered.

"It's the ship!" Gavin replied. *"It's happening! It's really happening! It's turning into a ghost ship!"*

"I think we've already figured that out," Brian said.

"We've got to get out of here!" Gavin said. His voice was tense, with a renewed sense of urgency. "We've got to get out of here before it's too late!"

It might already be too late, I thought, but I pushed the idea away.

"There's a door," Gavin said, and began walking toward it. The door was made of steel, and it was closed. Instead of a doorknob, however, there was a big, round wheel, also made of steel or iron.

Gavin grabbed the wheel and turned it.

Or, he *tried* to, anyway. The wheel wouldn't budge an inch.

"This one's locked," he said.

We looked around, searching for another door. We could still hear the ghostly moaning and groaning, and the rattling of chains. The sounds

71

seemed to be coming from every direction. It was eerie.

"There's a ladder over there," Brian pointed. Not far away was a series of metal rungs that ran up a wall to yet another closed door with a big wheel.

The three of us hurried over to it. Brian scrambled up the ladder. When he reached the door, he grasped the wheel.

"This one's locked, too," he said with a grimace. Then he climbed back down.

Gavin scratched his head. "This is weird," he said. "These doors were open a while ago. Now they're closed and locked."

Suddenly there was a loud *clang!* from the other side of the engine room. The sound was loud, and the three of us jumped.

"What was that?!?!" Brian gasped.

"I'll give you one guess," Gavin said.

"I know what it was," I said somberly. "It was the door that we came through. It just closed."

And I was right.

We hurried back through the engine room, around the big engines, up and down small stairs.

The door that we'd entered was closed.

Not only was it closed—but it was *locked*.

We were trapped in the engine room!

We searched and searched, but all of the doors were closed.

And locked.

There was no way out.

"Now what?" I asked. I was starting to get scared—even more scared than I had been before.

Gavin shook his head. "It looks like the doors have been locked from the other side," he said. "There's no way we'll be able to get them open."

"There has to be another way out," Brian said. "We've just got to find it."

Above and around us, the strange sounds continued. We could hear creaking, moans, rattling of chains, and, every so often, terrible laughter. It was horrible. I could only imagine what was going on in other parts of the ship.

I closed my eyes and hung my head.

Think, Emilee, I thought. *Think hard.*

I kept my eyes closed, trying to block out the rattling of chains and the ghostly sounds that echoed through the room.

Then, I opened my eyes and looked through the grate flooring beneath my feet. I could see the room below, cluttered with lots of steel boxes and other things. I could also see a slick of oil that looked to be in a vat or a drum of some kind.

That's it! I thought suddenly. *That's our way out of here!*

"Down there!" I exclaimed. I pointed down. "That's another room down there! Maybe if we could get down there, through the grate, we could find another way out of here!"

Gavin's eyes lit up. "It's worth a shot," he said. He tapped the floor with his right foot. "But I don't know if this grating is meant to move."

"It *must,*" I replied. "Or else, why would they put it here in the first place? There must be some way to get down there."

I got down on my hands and knees and reached my fingers through the grate. The metal felt cold and slick.

But it didn't move. In fact, it was pretty solid.

"Let's all look," I said. "There's got to be a grate that's loose or something."

Brian and Gavin dropped to their knees, and they, too, began feeling around, trying to find a grate that might be loose.

Soon, we had all gone off into different directions, each of us trying to find a way through the metal flooring . . . which, hopefully, would lead to a way out.

We searched and searched—until Brian suddenly began shouting.

"Here!" he exclaimed. "Right here! This whole section of metal grate is loose! Check it out!"

I leapt to my feet and raced to where Brian was kneeling.

He was on his knees. In his hands, he held a section of grate. In front of him, the floor opened up in a perfect square where he'd removed the piece of metal flooring.

"Great going, Brian!" I shouted, and my voice bounced around the engine room.

"There's even a ladder!" Gavin said. "There are metal rungs built into the wall leading down!"

Brian swung the metal grate to the side and dropped it. It clanged loudly, and the banging echoed through the engine room.

"Who's first?" I asked.

"I'll go," Brian said. "I found it, so I'll go down first."

Which was pretty brave, considering that my brother is kind of chicken when it comes to things like this. He's always the one that is daring someone else to do something. It's easier than doing it himself.

Brian squirmed through the square hole in the grating.

"Be careful," I said. "Don't fall."

"I won't," he replied.

Then he slipped beneath the grate. Gavin and I could see him as he grasped the metal rungs that were welded to the wall.

He paused before he reached the floor and looked around.

"I think I see a door over there!" he exclaimed. "And it looks open! I think we can get out of here!"

My spirits soared. I had started thinking that we were going to be trapped on the ship forever. Maybe we'd get out of here, after all.

Brian lowered himself down another rung.

"It is!" he shouted. "I can see an open door!"

He went down one more rung . . . .

And then he started screaming!

Brian's screams were terrible. I remember once, when he was in first grade, he was stung by a bee. He screamed like crazy!

This time, his screams were just as bad. He was clinging to the metal rungs, holding on for dear life, and screaming his head off.

"What?!?!" I shouted. "What's the matter?!?!"

"A spider!" Brian shouted back. *"It's on the wall! Ahhhh!"*

"Oh, for Pete's sake!" I said, rolling my eyes. "That's what you're screaming about?!?! I thought you were hurt, or maybe you saw one of those zombie things."

"This is a lot worse!" Brian squealed.

"Is he kidding?" Gavin whispered. *"Is he really* that *afraid of spiders?"*

I nodded. "He's been freaked out by spiders since he was a little kid. I don't know why."

I leaned way over and poked my head through the hole. My brother was only a few feet below.

"Brian!" I ordered. "Get a grip! It's just a spider! It's not going to hurt you! Now . . . keep going, so Gavin and I can come down, too!"

It took a moment for Brian to move. Finally, he started to climb down, but he kept glancing up at the spider, making sure that the thing wasn't coming after him.

I slipped through the grating, grabbed the metal rungs, and climbed down the ladder. On the wall was a spider, all right—but it was only about the size of a penny. I couldn't believe my brother had been so freaked out by such a dinky little thing.

Gavin followed me, and in no time at all, the three of us were in the area beneath the engine room. The air felt really thick and clammy, and I could smell old oil and musky, damp steel. Down here, there were no lights anywhere, but the lights from above splintered through the grating, so it was easy to see. It was just a little darker than the engine room above.

"Where is that door you talked about?" Gavin asked.

"Over there," Brian said. He pointed.

On the other side of the room was a small door. It was open, and I could see steps on the other side . . . steps that went *up*.

And that was *good*.

We needed to go up. We needed to go up—and *out*. I wanted out of this place and off this bizarre boat as fast as possible.

Down here, even beneath the engine room, we could still hear the weird rattling of chains and the haunting moans and groans coming from above.

"Let's get out of here," I said, motioning toward the open door. "I don't care where that leads to. We just have to get out of here, and off this ship!"

The floor beneath us was metal, unlike the grating that we'd walked on in the engine room. I had the feeling that we were at the very bottom of the ship.

And it wasn't a good feeling. It was a lonely, isolated feeling.

Cold.

Alone.

If we were at the bottom of the ship, that meant that we would have to find our way up and out.

Which, of course, would mean trying to keep away from those weird zombie sailors.

Boy, I thought. *When we get off of this boat, nobody is going to believe us. No one is going to believe that we were stranded on a ghost ship with zombie sailors.*

That is, of course, *if* we were able to get out of this ship alive. If the legends were true, we would be stuck here forever.

"Let's go," Gavin said. "Let's see where those stairs lead."

It was the only thing we could do.

We had no idea what we would find at the top of the steps . . . but we were about to find out.

Gavin led the way up the metal steps, followed by me, then Brian. There were two railings on either side of the stairway, and I gripped them tightly as we ascended. We could still hear the ghostly moans and strange sounds, but they were muffled and dull.

"See anything up there?" I asked Gavin.

"Not yet," he replied. "It's too dark."

Finally, he reached the top of the steps and passed through the open door. I was next, followed by Brian.

The room was dark, but Gavin fumbled around and found a switch on the wall. Instantly, bright, white light burst forth from two florescent tubes on the ceiling.

We were in what appeared to be some sort of storage chamber. The walls and ceiling were gray, and there were rows of steel shelves against the walls. The shelves held cans, boxes, jars, and other odds and ends. There was a door on the opposite wall, but when Gavin tried it, it was like all of the others: locked.

"Another dead end," Brian said. "We're never going to get out of here."

"Not so fast," I said, nodding to a large vent on the wall. "Take a look at that."

Behind one of the shelves was a big, square grate, about two feet wide and two feet high. It looked like an ordinary heating vent that we have in our house . . . except this one was a lot bigger.

"That looks like it might be some kind of vent," I said, pointing. "If that's the case, it has to lead somewhere."

"Yeah, probably the furnace," Brian said.

Gavin shook his head. "It's too big for that," he said. "I think it's an air vent. I think I remember my uncle pointing one out when I was on the ship once before. It's just a vent that helps circulate the air."

"So, that means that it *must* lead to another room!" I exclaimed.

"Even better!" Gavin said, nearly shouting. "It might even lead outside! To the main deck!"

Now, we were really excited.

"Let's get this stuff off the shelves," I said, as I began removing items and placing them on the floor. "Then, we can pull the shelf away from the wall. That grate must come off somehow. We can climb through the vent and make our escape!"

We got to work, removing items from the shelves, hoping to remove the grate and tunnel through the vent . . . to freedom.

How were we supposed to know that we were only moments away from disaster?

It only took a few minutes to remove the cans and boxes from the shelves. Finally, the entire rack was empty.

"Let's pull this shelf out of the way," Gavin said. "It doesn't look like it's too heavy."

And it wasn't. The three of us were easily able to pull the shelving unit away from the wall and push it aside.

We inspected the vent cover. It was made of metal and held to the wall by four screws. One of the screws was loose, and I was able to remove it with my fingers. The other screws were tight . . . but that didn't pose a problem, either. One of the things that we'd removed from the shelves was a screwdriver, and Gavin used it to unscrew the remaining three screws. I helped him with the metal vent cover, which came off the wall with only a little effort.

Sure enough, behind the grate was a vent, a square-shaped tunnel that was made of shiny sheet metal.

"Now," Gavin said confidently, "let's get out of here." He didn't even hesitate before pulling himself into the vent.

"Are you sure we're doing the right thing?" Brian asked quietly, as Gavin was climbing in.

I shook my head. "No," I replied. "No, I'm not sure at all. All I know is that I want off of this ship, and if I have to climb through a vent to do it, then that's what I'm going to do."

When Gavin was all the way into the vent, I climbed in after him. There was plenty of room to move, but, of course, we would have to crawl through the vent on our hands and knees, as there wasn't near enough room to stand. In fact, it was easier just to wriggle along on my belly, pulling myself along with my hands and pushing with my knees and feet.

"How are you guys doing?" Gavin asked from ahead of me. His voice sounded hollow and strange, with an odd echo.

"I'm fine," I replied, as I squirmed along the cold metal.

"Yeah, me, too," Brian said from behind me.

"It's getting kind of dark," Gavin said.

And he was right. The farther we got from the vent opening, the darker it became. Soon, it was so dark that we couldn't see anything. I could hear Gavin ahead of me and Brian behind me . . . and I could still hear those strange, ghostly sounds. They were very faint, like they were far away, but they were still there, a constant reminder that this was no joke: something was really wrong with this ship, and we had to get away.

We kept crawling through the darkness. All the while, I wondered where the vent would take us.

And I began to get nervous.

Maybe we hadn't done the right thing, after all. Maybe the vent would lead us right to where a bunch of those ugly zombie sailors were.

Don't even think about that, Emilee, I told myself. *Just think about getting off this ship.*

"Can you see anything yet?" I asked.

"Not yet," Gavin said. "It's still too dark. I have no idea where—"

Suddenly, Gavin's sentence was cut short.

In the next instant, he was screaming! He was screaming, but his voice faded away quickly.

"Gavin!" I shouted, and my voice echoed through the metal vent.

There was no answer.

But when I moved ahead a little and felt around with my hands, I knew why Gavin had screamed. I knew what had happened.

The vent made a sharp turn downward, like a slide. In the darkness, Gavin hadn't seen it, and he slid down, unable to stop himself.

Gavin had vanished!

17.

"What happened?" Brian asked. His voice echoed through the vent, and he sounded scared.

"Gavin slid down the vent!" I shrieked. "He's gone!"

Brian gasped.

"Gavin?!?!" I shouted. "Gavin, can you hear me?!?!" My voice echoed through the vent, but it faded quickly. I called out again: "Gavin?!?!"

And suddenly:

"I'm okay!"

It was Gavin!

His voice boomed through the vent, and he sounded far away.

"It's okay!" he shouted. "Go ahead and slide down the vent!"

"Are you sure?" I shouted back.

"Of course I'm sure!" Gavin replied. "I was scared at first, but the vent curves up, and comes out in a room. It's dark, but you won't get hurt!"

I was a little scared, and for good reason. I didn't like the idea of sliding down a vent, not knowing where I was going to end up.

But Gavin was okay. If he was okay, then I would be okay.

"Here I come!" I shouted. I pulled myself forward—and slid down the vent. Suddenly, it was like I was on a water slide . . . without the water, of course. The vent twisted and turned, and I felt like I was dropping almost straight down.

And it wasn't that scary, either. Now that I knew that Gavin was okay, it was actually kind of fun.

Soon, however, the vent turned upward, and I began to slow. In the next instant, I stopped.

"See?" I heard Gavin's voice in the darkness. He sounded very close. "You're fine. But it was a little scary for me, at first."

"Where are you?" I asked. I crawled forward a little, waving my right arm, only to find that, in front of me, the vent was gone. In the darkness, a hand grasped my arm.

"Right here," Gavin said, as he helped me out of the vent. I had just stood up when I heard a heavy, swishing sound. It grew louder, then stopped.

"Hey," Brian's voice echoed from the vent. "That was kind of fun!"

It was impossible to see him, of course, so I reached into the darkness until I felt him at the mouth of the vent.

"Here," I said, grabbing his arm and helping him out. "Stand up."

"Where are we?" Brian asked.

"I don't know," Gavin replied. "Somewhere near the bottom of the ship."

"Let's find a light," I said. "There has to be another way out of here besides the vent."

We stumbled around in the dark for a few moments. I stayed close to the wall, feeling around for a light switch.

"I found one!" Brian said from behind me.

Suddenly, the room lit up. Once again, we found ourselves in yet another storage room, similar to the room where we had been. There were several shelves on a far wall; some large, fifty-gallon drums; and what appeared to be old clothing, folded and piled in a corner.

Then, I noticed something on one of the shelves.

My eyes widened.

My heart pounded.

My arm shot out, and I pointed.

"Gavin! Brian!" I gasped. "Look at that!"

On the shelf was a radio!

Not a radio that plays music, but a two-way radio, with a microphone!

"A radio!" Gavin exclaimed. "That's just what we need! We can radio for help!"

We bounded across the room to the shelf . . . and our hearts sank.

The radio was broken. The back of it was missing, and there were broken wires coming out of it. Gavin tried turning it on, but, of course, it didn't work.

"Well, so much for that idea," Brian said in despair.

"There's a door over there," Gavin said, pointing. "Let's see where it goes."

Thankfully, the door wasn't locked, and I slowly pulled it open. My eyes darted around, looking for any zombie sailors. I didn't see any. The only thing I saw were metal steps leading up to a landing with yet another closed door.

"Finally," I said with relief. "Let's get out of here."

"Let's be careful," Gavin said. "We have no idea where those freaky zombies are."

Slowly, I started up the steps, followed by Gavin and Brian. When we reached the landing, I grasped the doorknob. Once again, I was relieved to find another door that wasn't locked.

"Be careful, Emilee," Brian said.

"I will," I replied, and I turned the knob and slowly pushed open the door.

It was another room. However, unlike most of the rooms we'd discovered, this one was very big, and was packed with all kinds of things. Mostly clothing on hangers, but there were other things, too. Hundreds of cables and wires snaked across the ceiling and up and down the walls. There were other gadgets and things that I hadn't a clue about. Some of them looked like machines or motors of some sort. There were nearly a dozen fire extinguishers along a wall, and several large closets with open doors. Although the room was pretty big, it sure was packed with a lot of stuff.

"Man," Brian said. "Just how big *is* this ship?"

"I don't care," Gavin said. "As long as we don't see any more of those zombie things."

Gavin spoke too soon. As soon as he uttered those words, we heard footsteps.

On the other side of the room, I saw movement.

A zombie sailor was coming!

We had to hide, and we didn't have much time. If we tried to go back through the door and down the stairs, I was sure the zombie would see us.

However, we could duck down and crawl behind some barrels, and maybe—*maybe*—get into one of the closets without being discovered.

I dropped to my knees, not even discussing my plan with Gavin or Brian. Hopefully, they would see what I had in mind, and follow.

And they did. I scurried along the cold floor and into the closet. I could hear Gavin and Brian behind me . . . but I could also hear the footsteps of the approaching zombie, getting closer and closer.

As quickly and quietly as I could, I slipped into the closet. Gavin and Brian were right behind me, and we nestled into a dark corner.

I peered up carefully, looking for the hideous creature, and got an unexpected surprise: the zombie had stopped and was looking at something on the other side of the room!

I reached out, grabbed the doorknob, and pulled the door closed as quietly as possible. Thankfully, it made no sound at all.

We were in complete darkness, except for a thin band of light coming from the bottom of the door. My heart was pounding like crazy.

How long is this going to go on for? I wondered. *Are we ever going to be able to escape?* It seemed like anywhere we went on the ship, we ran into those awful zombie sailors.

And I also knew that, sooner or later, we were going to be caught by them . . . if we weren't careful.

On the other side of the closet door, I heard footsteps again. The zombie was moving, and he was coming closer and closer.

What if he needs something from this closet? I thought. And then I thought: *why would a zombie need something from a closet?*

Everything was very confusing, but it didn't matter. What mattered was the footsteps that were getting closer, and closer, and closer . . .

They stopped right in front of the closet door, and I held my breath. Behind me, Gavin and Brian were perfectly still and silent.

After a moment, the footsteps shuffled away, then vanished altogether. We remained silent for a long time, sitting in the dark closet. My heart wasn't racing as fast as it had been.

"That was close," I whispered.

"Man, I thought that thing was going to open up the closet door and find us!" Brian said quietly. *"We would have had no place to go!"*

We waited for a few minutes. Finally, after we were sure that the zombie sailor was gone, I reached out to open the closet door.

I found the knob, and turned it.

Or, I *tried* to turn it.

But it wouldn't turn!

I pushed on the door, but it didn't budge.

I jiggled the doorknob and tried to turn it in both directions.

"What's wrong?" Gavin asked.

"The door!" I gasped. "It's . . . it's locked! We can't get out!"

20

As you can imagine, this nightmare we were living was getting worse by the second. Not only were we trapped on a real ghost ship with weird, zombie-like creatures . . . but now, we were locked in a closet!

"Good going, Sis," Brian sneered.

"Hey, I didn't know it would lock!" I snapped back. I was still jiggling the knob in hopes that, somehow, the door would unlock and open.

But, of course, that didn't work. I pushed on the door and tried to force it open, but it held fast.

"Well, we might not be able to get out," Gavin said, "but at least the zombies can't get us."

"Not unless they have a key," I said.

"Maybe we could find something to break the doorknob," Brian suggested.

Suddenly, I knew that Brian's idea might work! If we could find something in the closet—something like a hammer—we might be able to break the doorknob . . . and the lock! We'd be free!

But we'd have to find something first. And then we'd have to make sure that we listened for footsteps. The last thing we wanted would be for the zombie sailors to know where we were hiding.

"That's a good idea, Brian!" I said. "Let's see if we can find something to break the doorknob!"

Searching was difficult, because the only light in the closet was the thin band coming from beneath the door. I felt around for a light switch, but I didn't find any.

"I found a shoe," Gavin said, "but I don't think it'll work."

"Keep looking," I said. "There has to be something here."

We searched and searched. Mostly, the only things we found were articles of clothing. Some of it was folded in piles. Still other garments were hanging on hooks.

"This isn't looking good," Gavin said. "I don't think there's anything in here that we'll be able to use to break the doorknob."

"There's got to be a way out of here," I said. "We have to think positive."

"That's what Mom always says," Brian smirked, "but she's never been locked in a closet on a freaky ghost ship."

"Okay, let's try something else," Gavin said. "Let's search the pockets of all the clothing in here. It's a long shot, but maybe we'll find a key."

"Why would someone leave a key to the closet in the clothing?" Brian asked.

"I don't know," Gavin replied. "But we've got to try everything. Come on . . . let's start going through pockets."

And that's what we did. We searched through all of the clothing, going through pocket after pocket. I found a small amount of change, but nothing else.

No keys.

"I found a quarter," Gavin said. "That's not going to help."

"I found a paper clip," Brian said. "Anybody got any paper they need to keep together?"

Wait a minute!

"You . . . you found a paper clip?" I asked.

"Yeah," he said, laughing. "But it's not going to break the doorknob, that's for sure!"

"Brian . . . maybe we won't have to break the doorknob! Maybe we can use the paperclip to pick the lock!"

"Emilee!" Gavin gasped. "You're right! I've seen that on television before! We might be able to pick the lock!"

"Give me the paperclip," I said to Brian. In the darkness, he reached out. I found his hand and the paperclip between his fingers. I worked with it for a moment, straightening the clip so that there was about an inch-long point that I could use to insert into the lock.

"There," I said. "Let's give it a try!"

Now, I've never picked a lock before, and I really didn't have any idea how to do it . . .but I didn't even get a chance to try.

Suddenly, there was the sound of scuffling feet from the other side of the door.

And a deep, growling voice.

"Who's there?!?!"

A shadow fell over the thin band of light that was coming from beneath the closet door.

A zombie sailor! He'd heard us talking, and he knew where we were hiding!

21

We instantly fell silent.

Except, of course, for the beating of our hearts, which were hammering a mile a minute!

"I heard something," the zombie sailor growled. "I know you're in here somewhere!"

Gulp!

We stood in the darkness of the closet, unmoving and silent. I noticed that I was shaking all over, and I almost dropped the paperclip.

The doorknob jiggled, and I jumped. The three of us, however, stayed quiet.

The footsteps moved away. I heard another closet door open, and then a shuffling of boxes or crates.

The footsteps moved again, moving farther away.

We waited.

"Do . . . do you think he's gone?" Brian whispered, after we hadn't heard anything for several minutes.

"I . . . I think so," I said.

Slowly, I reached out with the paperclip. Then I stopped to listen, just to make sure I didn't hear anything.

Nothing.

It only took me a second to find the keyhole and insert the paperclip into it. I worked it around, not exactly sure what I was doing, or if I was doing it right.

"Is it working?" Gavin asked quietly.

"I don't know," I said. "I can't see what I'm doing, and I'm not sure I know what to do, anyway."

At that moment, I heard a sound.

Not a footstep, or anything like that.

It was a solid *click!*

And it sounded like it came from the lock.

I pulled the paperclip from the keyhole. Then, I grabbed the doorknob . . . and pushed.

The closet door opened!

Light streamed in, and I squinted and partially covered my eyes with one hand. The light seemed very, very bright.

"Emilee!" Brian exclaimed. "You did it! You really did!"

"Shhhh!" Gavin warned, placing a finger to his lips. "Just in case there are any more of those creatures around!"

I pushed the door further, and I frantically glanced all around the large room.

No zombie sailors. Whew!

We stepped out of the closet. Again, I could hear the strange sounds coming from somewhere above. While we had been locked in the closet, we couldn't hear them, but now I could make out the dragging chains and the ghostly moans and wails.

"Let's go that way," I said, pointing. "That's where we saw the zombie sailor when we first came into this room. He had to come from somewhere."

"You want to find one of those creepy things?!?!" Brian gasped.

"Of course not," I replied. "But he had to come from somewhere. Let's find out where . . . and get off this ship!"

I led the way, and we wound down a long, gray corridor that ended at a stairway.

And I couldn't help but notice that the horrifying sounds were getting louder.

Wherever we were going, we were getting closer to the source of those sounds.

"There's a door at the top of the steps," Gavin said. "I'm not sure where we are, but we must be close to the main deck. That door might even take us there."

Slowly, we ascended the metal stairs.

We reached the door.

Now, one thing that really bothered me was that the door didn't have any window. We couldn't see through to the other side, so we had no idea what lay beyond.

But we had to find out. We had no other choice, if we wanted to find a way off the ship.

Like other doors we'd encountered, this one didn't have a regular knob, but a big wheel. I grabbed it with both hands, and turned it.

The door began to swing open.

I gasped.

So did Gavin and Brian.

Because right then and there, we knew that there was no way out.

If there were any doubts that we were on a ghost ship, they were erased the moment we opened the door.

The first thing I saw were spider webs. They were everywhere: in the corners, on the ceiling, and on the walls. There was an old dresser on the far wall, covered with dust and more spider webs. On it was a skull . . . and inside the skull was a glowing candle!

All three of us gasped at the exact same time, but we were too afraid to speak. We just kept staring.

On another wall, near the ceiling, was a row of sleeping bats. They were about four inches long, and they were hanging upside down.

There was a table near the same wall, and on it was another skull with a candle. Still another candle was burning next to it.

Old pictures adorned the walls, too. They were covered with dust. One picture was that of a zombie sailor. But another one was altogether different. It was a picture of an old sea captain, and he looked crusty and haggard. He had a gray beard, and he was smoking a pipe. His eyes seemed to glow, and I knew right away that this must be the captain that Gavin spoke about.

"It's really, really true," Gavin said quietly. His voice was trembling with fear. *"All of the stories and legends. All of them are true."*

However, by far the scariest thing in the room was the large, dark, wooden box that lay in the middle of the floor, near the table.

A coffin!

The very same coffin that the two zombie sailors had been carrying a short time ago!

"What's that thing doing here?" I asked.

"I don't know," Gavin replied, shaking his head slowly. "And I'm not sure if I *want* to know."

We had been so caught up in looking around the room that we hadn't noticed that the ghostly sounds had stopped. Suddenly, they started up again, louder than before. They sounded like they were coming from right above us.

Brian pointed to a closed door on the other side of the room. Like several other doors, it had a large wheel that opened it.

"Maybe w . . . we . . . c . . . c . . . can . . . g . . . g . . . get out through th . . . th . . . there," he stammered. He was really scared.

"Maybe that will just lead us to a room full of zombie sailors," Gavin said.

"Well, there's no other way out that we've found," I said. "We have to at least see what's on the other side."

"You first," Brian said.

I shrugged, trying to be brave. "Sure," I said, but, truthfully, I wasn't sure at all. I had no idea what was on the other side of the door. Besides . . . for all we knew, it might be locked. It might be another dead end.

But we wouldn't know unless we tried.

I began walking slowly.

"I'll go with you," Gavin said, and he, too, began walking across the floor. Brian decided that he wasn't going to be left alone and fell in behind us.

And, while I didn't want to get anywhere near the coffin, there was just no way around it. The coffin was in the middle of the room. The table was on one side of it, and the old dresser on the other. As I got closer to the long, rectangular box, I tried not to think about what might be inside.

In two more steps, I was right beside the coffin.

That's when it happened.

There was a slight squeaking sound, and a scrape.

I stopped.

Then I looked down at the coffin . . . and screamed.

The coffin lid was opening . . . all by itself! Something was coming out of the coffin!

23

Have you ever been so scared that you couldn't move?

Well, me, too . . . but I was past that, this time. I mean . . . I was so scared that my legs moved without even thinking!

I turned and raced to the other side of the room. Gavin and Brian were right behind me, and they ran into me when I stopped.

We turned to look at the horrible sight . . . and it was worse than I imagined.

Inside the coffin was a skeleton! It had pushed the coffin lid up with a long, gray, bony arm and was holding it there, half open. It was the grossest thing I have ever seen in my life.

We watched in horror and confusion. What should we do? Where could we go?

Suddenly, the lid of the coffin slammed shut with a heavy *bang!* Gavin, Brian, and I jumped.

I wasn't waiting another second. I grabbed the cold, metal wheel on the door and turned.

I heaved a sigh of relief when I realized that the door wasn't locked. If it had been locked, we would have had no other choice but to go back to the other side of the room—past the coffin—and back to where we came from.

I pushed the door slowly, and it opened without a sound.

But, we were in for yet another shock: the room that we were looking at had transformed, just like the room we were standing in! There wasn't a coffin on the floor, but the room looked just as spooky, with spider webs and skulls and all sorts of scary things.

And it was dark, too. There was only one candle lit, and it didn't give off much light at all.

But one thing I was glad to see:

On the far side of the room was a door . . . and it was wide *open!* I had no idea where it might lead, but as long as we were finding open doors, we were doing well.

The problem was, there was something waiting for us in this next room.

Something hairy.

And black.

Something that was about to attack.

We walked through the door and into the next room. I knew we weren't out of danger yet, by far, but I sure was glad to be away from that coffin and that creepy skeleton!

The room we were now in was filled with all kinds of old furniture, and there was dust on everything. Earlier, all of the rooms in the ship had been filled with equipment and machines and clothing—things that were necessary for the crew.

Now, it was all gone, replaced by old desks and chairs. Spider webs hung from everything, and I couldn't help but think that it was like walking through a haunted house.

We started across the room slowly, tiptoeing. I wanted to run, but I also didn't want to attract any attention. After all . . . we had no idea where any of those weird zombies might be.

And I definitely wanted to see them before they saw us!

"We've got to be near the main deck," Gavin said, looking upward to the ceiling. "I think those sounds and noises are coming from there."

"But just what is making the noises?" I asked. "I mean . . . I don't want to go if there are a bunch of zombie sailors up there!"

"It might be our only way out," Gavin said.

"Maybe we could jump overboard, into the water," Brian suggested.

"We could," Gavin replied, "if we got that far. But the water is going to be really cold."

"I don't care," Brian said. "I'll take the cold water before I take being on this ship forever."

When we got near the middle of the room, we stopped. I leaned sideways, trying to peer through the open door ahead of us. I wanted to make sure that there were no zombies waiting for us.

"I don't see anything," I whispered.

"Me neither," Gavin said, shaking his head.

Brian was behind us. "What's that thing?" he asked.

I turned, and so did Gavin. Brian was pointing to a dark corner. There was something there, tucked up near the ceiling, about twenty feet from where we were standing. It was big, whatever it was.

"Beats me," Gavin said with a shrug. "Why?"

"I . . . I thought I saw it move," Brian said.

"It's probably nothing," I said. But the more I looked at it, and the more my eyes adjusted to the dim light, I began to see features.

Of a long, spiny leg.

A thick, furry body, the size of a beach ball.

And I know this is going to sound crazy—but it looked like . . . .

A spider.

A *giant* spider.

"Are . . . are you . . . seeing what . . . what I'm seeing?" I stammered. My eyes never left the dark shadow in the corner.

"I think I see something," Gavin replied, "but I don't believe it."

"Seeing is believing," I said, "and I think I see a super huge spider."

Now that someone had spoken the word—spider—we were filled with terror. Brian was so terrified that he couldn't move or speak. He was afraid of even the smallest of spiders . . . a gigantic one like this was probably going to freak him out for life!

I took a step toward the spider. That's right: *toward* the spider. I was sure that what I was seeing couldn't be real.

But, then again, the zombie sailors were real. And the skeleton in the coffin. And the bats hanging on the wall in the other room.

I suddenly realized that I had made a terrible mistake.

In the dark corner, a leg moved.

And another.

Then another.

And another!

Suddenly, the spider was moving, crawling down the wall, reaching out with long, wiry legs.

It was coming after us!

When the spider reached the floor, we panicked.
Up until that point, we had been really scared by
a lot of things . . . but there was nothing that could
have prepared us for being attacked by a giant,
vicious spider!

Then I remembered something:

When I was in Saginaw, Michigan, last year,
visiting my cousin, Jared Rook, he told me how he
and a few of his friends had battled giant spiders.
I didn't believe him at the time.

Now, seeing the enormous, black, hairy thing in the corner of the dark room made me realize that my cousin had been telling the truth, after all!

The three of us spun and bolted for the door. We were so frantic that we almost knocked each other over! We couldn't get out of there fast enough.

At this point, I guess I didn't care if we saw another zombie sailor. I just wanted away from that spider . . . the faster, the better.

We ran across the room and through the open door.

And, as fate would have it, we *did* see a zombie.

He was standing at the end of a long hall . . . but he was looking the other way! He hadn't spotted or heard us . . . yet.

Without a word, I pointed to yet another door that was open, with stairs leading down. Although I didn't want to go deeper into the ship, it seemed like the best place at the moment. If that zombie turned, he'd spot us right away.

Unless we went down the stairs.

Brian and Gavin saw where I was pointing, and they nodded. I led the way, and we tiptoed down the metal stairs.

Then we stopped.

We looked around . . . and we couldn't believe our good luck.

26

The room was filled with electronics, but, most importantly:

Radios!

There were several two-way radios on a desk, and one mounted on a wall.

"One of these has got to work!" Gavin said. He darted to the wall, plucked the microphone from the radio, and turned on the power button. Red and green lights blinked and flashed.

"Yes!" I exclaimed triumphantly, and then I shot a nervous glance over my shoulder, just to make sure that there were no zombie sailors coming down the steps.

"Try it!" Brian said. "Say something!"

Gavin pressed a button on the microphone. "Hello?" he said. "Can anyone hear me? Hello?" Then he released the button.

We waited. After a few moments went by with no response, Gavin tried again.

"Hello?" he repeated. "Can anyone hear me? This is an emergency! We need help!"

The seconds ticked slowly past. With every passing moment, our hopes faded.

Then:

"This is the captain of the Sea Lady. What's your emergency?"

"What's the 'Sea Lady'?" Brian asked.

"It's the name of a boat!" Gavin said excitedly. Then he pressed the microphone button again, and raised it to his mouth. "We're trapped on the Coast Guard cutter!" he exclaimed. "Only, it's not the Coast Guard cutter anymore! It's a ghost ship, with zombies and skeletons and giant spiders!"

He let go of the button, and we waited. After a few moments, the radio sputtered.

"This is Sea Lady. Can you repeat, please?"

Again, Gavin spoke into the microphone. "It's true!" he said. "Me and my friends are trapped on a ghost ship! There are zombies everywhere, and we can't get out! We need help!"

A few seconds passed, and then the man's voice came over the speakers again.

"Listen . . . I don't know what you kids are up to, but you can get into big trouble screwing around with the radio!"

The three of us gasped.

"He thinks we're kidding!" I said.

Gavin spoke into the microphone. "Please, sir, this is no joke! We need help!"

Again, the man's voice came through the speaker. "This is your last warning. You can't be playing games and telling people you have an emergency when you don't! Now . . . if you do it again, I'm going to report you! Over and out!"

Gavin was about to say something into the microphone, but I stopped him. "Don't," I said. "He's not going to believe you."

"But if he reports us to someone, maybe they'll come and help us," Brian said.

I shook my head. "I doubt it," I replied. "No one knows where we are. They wouldn't begin to know where to look. Even if we told them we were on the Coast Guard cutter, they would probably think we were joking."

"You're right, Emilee," Gavin said, and he hooked the microphone back onto the radio. "In fact, we don't even know if the Coast Guard cutter even exists anymore."

"Well, it must," I said. "I mean . . . you wouldn't expect to find a radio on a ghost ship, would you?"

Gavin frowned. "I guess you're right," he said.

"So, now what?" Brian said with a shrug.

"I wish we had a map of the inside of the ship," Gavin said. "A map would at least show doors and rooms and exits."

"Too bad we can't sound the alarm or ring a bell," I said. "Someone might hear it and come to help."

Gavin's eyes grew wide. His jaw dropped.

"Emilee!" he exclaimed. "That's it! That's what we need to do!"

"What?" I asked.

"The alarm! If we can somehow make it to the bridge, we can sound the alarm! It'll be heard all over the ship . . . even on shore! It's really loud!"

"But Gavin," I began, "it might not even be there. Remember the rooms we just came from? They changed and weren't at all like the other rooms. What if the bridge has changed, too?"

"Well," Gavin said, "we don't have many options. We can try and find the bridge and sound the alarm. Even if we don't find it, or even if it's changed, we might still be able to find a way off the ship."

"What other options do we have?" Brian asked.

Gavin looked at my brother, then at me. "We can wait right here," he said. "We can wait . . . until the zombies find us."

That didn't sound very fun at all.

"All right," I said. "Let's keep going. If we find the bridge, we can sound an alarm."

"But maybe we'll find a way off the ship before we even find the bridge," Gavin said hopefully. "Maybe this whole thing will end soon."

Gavin was wrong.

It wasn't about to end.

In fact, in a matter of seconds, it was about to get a whole lot worse . . . .

On the other side of the radio room was yet another door. It occurred to me that the ship must be like some big maze, with doors and halls and rooms that all interconnect and lead to one another.

All we had to do was find the right door and the right hallway. It seemed like an easy thing to do, but you have to remember: the *Mackinaw* is very, very big. It would be easy for anyone to get lost on it.

Just as we had done.

As luck would have it, we were able to sneak through several rooms, up and down steps, and through narrow passageways without seeing any zombies. We didn't see anything strange. No spider webs, no bats, no giant spiders . . . and no zombies. If we hadn't seen those things with our very own eyes, I would have thought that we were on a normal ship.

But we continued to hear the strange, sinister sounds. They were a constant reminder that, at any moment, we might encounter a zombie sailor, or perhaps something else.

We walked in silence, slowly, our eyes darting to the left and to the right, on constant lookout for anything.

Until—

"Look!" Brian suddenly hissed. *"Look at that sign!"*

He was pointing ahead of us to a metal sign that was screwed into the wall next to a closed door. It was a metal plate with silver letters:

BRIDGE

"We did it!" Gavin exclaimed. "It's the bridge! We made it!"

"Yeah," I replied hesitantly, "but what's on the other side of the door?"

"What if a giant spider is there?" Brian asked, his face flushed with fear.

"It's a chance we have to take," Gavin said bravely. "The bridge is the brains of the ship. If we can't find a way out through there . . ."

He stopped short of finishing his sentence, because we all knew what he meant. On the other side of the door was the ship's bridge—our last chance. If we couldn't find a way out, or find a way to alert others, we would be on the Great Lakes Ghost Ship forever.

One thing we had noticed, however, is that the strange sounds—dragging chains, screaming, wicked, terrible laughter—had become louder. It seemed like it was coming from all around us . . .

and it seemed like it was coming from the bridge, too.

"Let's go for it," Gavin said.

He placed his hand on the doorknob, and turned it.

There was a click, and the door slowly opened.

The strange, haunted sounds streamed out, louder than before.

And when Gavin opened the door all the way, we couldn't have imagined what we were seeing.

23

What we saw in the bridge was shocking.

The room was dim, lit only by a few candles. There were spider webs everywhere: stretching from the ceiling to the walls, over tables and equipment, across everything. There were big spiders hiding in dark corners, although these spiders weren't nearly as big as the one we'd seen earlier, in another part of the ship.

The sounds had grown louder, too, and they seemed to come from all around us. I couldn't see just where, but the awful clinks of dragging chains and the terrible laughter that echoed through the room sent shivers up and down my spine.

And what's more:

The windows were completely covered up. I was sure that it must be dark outside by now, but the windows had been completely covered with old blankets and sheets. Spider webs clung to some of the cloth.

"It doesn't look like anyone's been here in over fifty years," Gavin whispered.

I was too freaked out to say anything. Brian was, too, as he had spotted the spiders on the wall and the ceiling, and he was frozen in terror.

But Gavin had been right.

On the wall was a large switch, and beneath it was a metal plate that read:

EMERGENCY ALARM

I couldn't believe it! There was a red, disc-shaped bell above the switch, covered with spider webbing.

"We found it!" I gasped suddenly. "Gavin! You were right! We found the alarm!"

Gavin reached out his hand. "Let's just hope it works," he said.

But just before he was about to grab the alarm, a door on the other side of the bridge opened.

The three of us jumped and turned.

In the doorway stood two zombie sailors!

"There you are!" one of them hissed. "We've been looking for you!"

"Run!" I shrieked, and the three of us turned around to go out the door that we'd come in through—

Only to find another zombie sailor blocking our way!

There was nowhere to go!

29

The zombie sailors, as you can probably imagine, looked hideous. Their faces were pasty-white, their lips were gray, and their eye sockets were almost black, making their eyes look sunken. They wore old, tattered sailor uniforms that were ripped and torn. Their hair was messy. One of them wore a hat, and it looked like a dog had been chewing on it.

"We've been looking for you for a while," one of the zombies said. "Now, we'll see what the captain has to say."

I shuddered. *The captain!* I thought. *No! The zombie sailors are bad enough! I don't want to see the captain!*

"Come with us," the zombie ordered.

No way, I thought. *If we go with them, we're goners. If we can get away, we're going to have to do it now.*

"Watch out!" I suddenly blurted, pointing past the zombie that was behind us. He turned . . . and it was the chance I needed.

I dove to the ground and quickly scrambled between his legs. Actually, it was easier than I thought, and before the zombie even knew what was going on, I was on my feet, through the door, and darting down the metal stairs. Brian had done the same . . . however, the zombie reached out and grabbed Brian's shirt sleeve. It ripped, and the zombie lost his grip. Brian sprang ahead, his mouth gaping wide, his bulging eyes filled with fear.

And, amazingly, Gavin was able to escape, too. While the zombie had been trying to catch my brother, Gavin had darted around behind him. When Brian's shirt tore, Gavin used the opportunity to leap. He grabbed the railing and slid all the way down the stairs, where he smacked into Brian and nearly knocked him over.

I was in the lead, running down a narrow hallway, headed for a door that would lead somewhere—anywhere—safe. Maybe we could again find someplace to hide, where we wouldn't be discovered.

But it wasn't going to happen.

Ahead of me, two zombie sailors suddenly appeared. At first, I thought they had just appeared out of thin air . . . and then I realized they had come through a door.

I stopped. Gavin and Brian ran into me.

"Why did you stop?!?!" Brian wailed. "The zombies are right behind us!"

I looked, and, sure enough, the zombie sailors that had nearly caught us in the bridge were running toward us.

But in front of us, there were two more zombie sailors, blocking our path.

Our luck had finally run out, and there was nowhere we could go.

30

The zombies behind us stopped running. They knew we couldn't escape.

"Now," one of them said, "if you're done playing games, we'll take you to the captain. He'll deal with you his way."

One of the zombies grabbed my arm, and I flinched and tried to shake him away. I didn't want his gross arm to be touching my skin!

But he held fast. Two zombies grasped Brian's and Gavin's arms, and they began to march us through the ship.

This is it, Emilee, I thought. *You're not getting out of this one.*

I wondered what our parents would do when we didn't return home. Would they suspect that we'd been taken aboard the ghost ship? Would we ever see them again?

I cried a teeny, tiny bit.

You would too, I bet, if you were in my shoes.

We wound through cold, gray hallways, through rooms, up and down metal stairs.

Finally, we reached a dark door. On the wall next to it was a name plate that read:

CAPTAIN'S QUARTERS
AUTHORIZED PERSONNEL ONLY

One of the zombies knocked, and a gruff voice from the other side answered.

"Come in!"

The zombie turned the doorknob and pushed the door open.

160

"Inside," one of the zombies ordered, and we were pushed gently into the captain's quarters.

Like the bridge, the room was dark and gloomy. A couple of candles burned. On the captain's desk was a glowing pumpkin, its face carved like that of a zombie. It was horrifying.

But about the captain himself:

He was wearing tattered clothing, similar to what the zombies were wearing, except the captain's clothing looked like it was some sort of old rain gear. His hair was gray and thick, and he had a thick mustache and beard. And he was wearing a hat, too, which was in equally poor condition.

"Well, well," he boomed, crossing his arms. His voice was deep and gravelly. "It seems like we've found our stowaways."

My teeth were chattering. My knees were knocking. I couldn't move or speak.

"Do you mind telling me just what you were doing on board?" the captain asked.

There was no way I could speak. Not yet, anyway. Maybe not ever. I was so scared, I didn't think I'd ever be able to say another word for as long as I lived . . . however long that would be.

"We . . . we were taking a tour," Gavin spluttered. "With my uncle. He had to go away. We saw . . . saw . . . one of . . . of these . . . these *things,* and we ran and hid."

"Why didn't you remain where you were?" the captain asked.

"We were scared," Gavin replied.

One of the zombies behind us snickered.

A snickering zombie? I thought. *Since when do zombies snicker? They're supposed to be dead.*

"So, you weren't trying to sneak on board?" the captain asked.

We all shook our heads. I was surprised that I was actually able to move at all.

"No," Gavin said. "My uncle is in the Coast Guard. He invited me and my friends on board for a tour. While we were on board, it changed into this ghost ship."

Behind us, the zombies laughed, and they didn't sound like zombies at all. I mean, you would expect zombies to be hissing and moaning and not saying much of anything.

Not these zombies. They were acting like this was all some big joke.

"What's going on here?" I asked. "Why were the zombies after us?"

"They weren't after you to harm you," the captain said. "You see, we couldn't get started until we'd found you. It would be too dangerous to have you three kids wandering the ship unsupervised."

"Couldn't get started doing what?" Brian squeaked.

"Why, haunting the ship," the captain said. "It's time for the haunting to begin!"

Oh no!

I shuddered.

Brian gasped. He covered his eyes with both hands. "I knew it!" he cried. "I knew it! We're stuck here forever, just like the legend!"

At this, the captain laughed, then he shook his head. "Oh, you've heard the story," he said, "about the Great Lakes Ghost Ship."

We all nodded.

"Well, there *is* such a thing," the captain said, "however, in reality, the 'ghost ship' is quite a bit different than the legend."

"What . . . what do you mean?" Brian stammered.

"We do this every year," the captain explained. "Every October, right around Halloween, we decorate the *Mackinaw* to look like a haunted house. The crew dresses up in costume . . . many of them zombies . . . and we invite people to come on board and tour our 'haunted' ship."

I couldn't believe what I was hearing.

"You mean that all of the things we saw were just decorations?" I asked.

The captain nodded. "That's right," he replied.

"But that's impossible!" Gavin said. "I mean . . . we saw a skeleton! It pushed open a coffin lid!"

"And a giant spider, too!" Brian blurted out. "He attacked us!"

Again, the zombies behind us roared with laughter. The captain smiled.

"No, those weren't real," he explained. "Those were just props with motion sensors. Did you realize that the coffin lid didn't open until you got close to it? And the giant spider? It, too, has a tiny motion detector. When it senses something move, it sets off the spider. The same with the skeleton in the coffin."

So that was it! I thought. I have a motion-sensor toy at home. It's a bunny, and when you get near it, it sings a silly song and dances a little bit.

"But what about the bats?" Gavin asked. "We saw a bunch of bats in one of the rooms."

"Just plastic," one of the zombies answered. "I bought them at the department store, along with the fake spider webs. And we're not real zombies! It's just make-up and old clothing!"

I couldn't believe what we were hearing! We'd been on the ship a few hours, and we really thought that we were on a 'haunted' ship! Instead, the Coast Guard cutter had just been made up to look haunted!

"That's why we've been trying to find you guys," one of the zombies explained. "You see, we had to lock off certain parts of the ship to keep people out. We don't decorate the whole ship . . .

only a few rooms. Gavin, your uncle had to go on an emergency run to help repair a small boat. He told us to let you know . . . but when we went to find you three, you were gone."

"And we did everything we could to hide from you," I said.

"You did a good job," the captain said. "We found you just in time. We are just about to let people inside, and, if we hadn't found you three, we would have had to cancel the festivities. Look out the window."

The three of us stepped over to a large, round window, and peered down.

It was dark, and the shipyard was lit up by bright white lights. On the docks we could see dozens and dozens of people, waiting to board the *Mackinaw*.

"They're all here to walk through the ship," the captain said. "We do this every year, and it's a lot of fun for everyone."

I couldn't believe it, but everything actually made sense. The ghostly sounds that we heard were just a compact disc that was played over the ship's loudspeakers. The 'zombies' were actually real Coast Guard officers, dressed to look that way.

When the captain found out that we hadn't meant any harm, he said that he was sorry that we'd been so frightened. He even offered to let us wander through the ship again, if we wanted to experience the haunted ship the way that it was meant to be.

"No thanks," Brian answered quickly. "I've had enough scares for one day."

"Yeah, thanks," I said, "but we should be getting home. I hope we didn't cause too much trouble."

The captain waved it off. "No trouble," he said. "Now . . . if you'll excuse me, I've got some haunting of my own to do."

And with that, the zombies turned and left. We followed them out, with the captain behind us.

That officially ended our nightmare aboard the Great Lakes Ghost Ship. I was so relieved to find out that the story Gavin told me wasn't true, and I was even more relieved when we left the ship and set our feet upon dry land.

But our night wasn't over just yet.

There was one more horrifying thing that was about to happen . . . something that made us realize that maybe—just maybe—the legend of the Great Lakes Ghost Ship is true after all.

It happened when we were almost home. We said goodnight to Gavin, and Brian and I were walking along the sidewalk, in the glow of the streetlights.

"That was the freakiest thing that has ever happened to me," he was saying. "I really thought those zombies were real."

"Me, too," I said. "I didn't think we would ever get off that ship."

"I'll bet it would have been a blast if we knew ahead of time that it was all for fun," Brian said.

"Yeah, but now that we know, maybe we can do it next year . . . and wait in line, like everyone else."

Ahead of us, from the shadows, a man appeared. Actually, I think he had been standing there, and when we got closer, we could see him. He was wearing a captain's costume, almost identical to the captain that we'd met on the *Mackinaw*. He was smoking a pipe and holding up a lantern.

"There's someone else with a cool costume," I said, as we drew closer to the man.

"Yeah," Brian agreed. "He looks just as freaky as the captain. Maybe even freakier."

We drew even closer. Still, the man never moved. He just stood there, puffing on his pipe and holding the lantern.

"That's a great costume," Brian said, as we approached the man. "You should be on the Coast Guard cutter."

The man said nothing. It was kind of weird.

Finally, when we were only a few feet away, the old man spoke.

"Come with me," he said, gently waving the lantern back and forth, *"come with me, and sail the seas. There's no need for fear, no need for fright . . . come with me, and sail into the night!"*

I laughed, and so did Brian.

"Hey, that's good," Brian said. "Did you make that up?"

"Come along and sail the sea," he said. Then he smiled a terrible smile. Smoke from his pipe drifted around his face. *"Yes, yes, children. Come along and sail the sea . . . come along, and be just like me!"*

Then he cackled and laughed, throwing his head back. Brian and I hurried on by, glad to be past him.

"That dude was weird," Brian whispered, as we hustled along the sidewalk. *"He was really, really weird."*

I turned to catch one more glance at the old sea captain.

But what I saw was something that I will never, ever forget for as long as I live . . . .

33

The old sea captain was fading away! He was vanishing . . . right before my eyes!

Brian had already turned around, and we watched as the old man's appearance grew faint. It was as if he had turned into smoke, and was drifting off into the night.

"I can't believe this!" I exclaimed. "This isn't real! This can't be happening!"

"Hey, I'm seeing it, too!" Brian said. "So it must be real!"

In seconds, the old sea captain was gone. Brian and I were the only ones on the street.

"Let's get out of here!" I exclaimed. We broke into a run and didn't stop until we reached the front porch of our grandparents' home.

As you can imagine, nobody believed us. Oh, they believed our story about being on the *Mackinaw* and getting scared by the zombies . . . but they didn't believe us about the old sea captain that had vanished into thin air. No matter what we said or how we said it, our parents and grandparents just smiled and shook their heads.

But Brian and I knew. We *knew* that we'd seen the old sea captain. We knew that the legend was true, after all.

Strange.

The next day, it was time to head back to Grand Blanc. We left around noon. The drive normally takes us about three hours . . . but not this particular day.

Right around Grayling, which is a small town just off I-75 in northern lower Michigan, our car just died.

For no reason.

"It's the sea captain," Brian said. "He's cursed our car."

"It's not the sea captain," Dad said, as he pulled the car to the shoulder of the road. "There is no such thing as ghosts."

Well, we wound up having to get the car towed to a service station in Grayling, where they told us it would take a couple of hours to fix.

Which was fine with me. Right across from the mechanic's garage was a park and a river. It would be fun to explore while the car was getting repaired.

Brian and I walked across the street. Downtown was busy, and there were lots of cars to watch for.

But there weren't too many people in the park. On the bank, not far away, was a boy about my age, and he was fishing. However, he wasn't using a regular fishing pole . . . he was using what's called a 'fly rod'. It's a longer rod, used to cast artificial flies. It's a lot different than regular fishing, but I've never done it before. Actually, it was kind of fun to watch.

When he took a break and set the rod in the grass, we walked up to him.

"Catching anything?" Brian asked.

The boy looked up. He had dark brown hair and lots of freckles, and his face was tanned by the sun.

"Naw," he said. "Nothing, yet."

I found out that his name was Craig Pierce, and he lived in Grayling, not far from town. He said that he fly fishes all the time, and he loves it. He even showed us some of the flies he used, which he made himself.

I was fascinated. "You . . . you *made* this?" I asked, holding up a small dry fly for inspection. It was about the size of a nickel, and it was made to float on the surface of the water to trick fish into thinking it was a *real* fly.

Craig nodded. "Yep," he replied. "I tie all of my own flies."

"What do you fish for?" I asked.

"Well, here in the AuSable River, I fish for trout. But a couple of weeks ago, I caught something that I couldn't believe. In fact, you wouldn't believe it, either."

"What did you catch?" Brian asked. "A shark?"

I frowned and rolled my eyes. "Don't be a goofball," I said. "There aren't any sharks in Michigan."

"Yeah, well, there aren't supposed to be alligators, either," Craig said, "but that's what I caught."

Brian and I just stared.

"Okay," I finally said with a laugh. "What's the joke?"

Craig shook his head. "It's no joke," he replied. "I couldn't believe it, either. But I caught an alligator. More than one, actually. Want to hear about it? It might take a while."

"Yeah," I said. "Our car is getting fixed, and we've got a couple of hours."

Craig sat down on the grass. Brian and I did the same.

"Okay," he began, "it all started when I was fishing one evening . . . ."

I listened closely, and, the more I heard, the more I realized that Craig wasn't making anything up! He really had caught an alligator in the AuSable River!

But when he explained some of the other things that happened, I realized that what he'd gone through was a lot scarier than what Brian and I had been through on the Coast Guard Cutter!

NEXT IN THE
MICHIGAN CHILLERS
SERIES:
#12: AUSABLE ALLIGATORS

TURN THE PAGE TO READ A FEW
SAMPLE CHAPTERS
FREE!

The final rays of sun bled through thick pine trees. Stars began to twinkle.

Perfect, I thought.

Around me, water babbled. I was in the middle of the AuSable River with my fly rod in hand.

Alone.

Even better. No crowds, no one to disturb my fishing.

My name is Craig Pierce, and I live in Grayling. Actually, we live out of town a bit. There are not many houses where we live . . . just forest. Lots of pine, oak, maple, quaking aspen, and cedar trees.

In fact, the nearest house is almost a quarter of a mile away. It belongs to the Penrose family. They live in Pontiac, which is about a four hour drive south. Heather Penrose is twelve, which is how old I am. In the summer, we fly fish together. She's pretty cool, and I wish she didn't live so far away.

Because I knew that she would love to be trout fishing tonight.

You see, the night was *perfect*. It was warm, and I was catching quite a few fish. Nothing big, yet . . . but that was about to change.

If there's one single thing that I love more than anything, it's fly fishing for trout. The AuSable River is a famous trout stream, with lots of brook trout and brown trout. My dad taught me how when I was nine, and I've fly fished ever since.

(Except in the winter, of course. Grayling gets a lot of snow in the winter, and it gets really cold!)

But during the summer, on nights like tonight, I was right at home. I was wearing my rubber waders, which come up to my chest and allow me to walk in the water without getting wet. I also had on my vest, which carried my fly boxes, leaders, a spare line, a small penlight, a net, and some insect repellant. That's another thing you need if you fly fish the AuSable: bug spray. The mosquitos and black flies will try to eat you alive.

But tonight, I would encounter something else that could quite possibly eat me alive.

Not a mosquito.

Not a black fly.

Not a snake or a lizard or anything else I could have possibly imagined.

In fact, if I would have known then what I know now, I probably wouldn't have set foot in the river.

A bat flitted past, spinning and squealing as it hunted down a bug. Water rippled, and I took a step downstream. Gravel crunched beneath my rubber-soled waders, and the sound was muted by the babbling river. A choir of crickets and frogs sang.

I cast my fly, laying out the line so that it skirted beneath the overhanging branches of a cedar tree. Fly fishing is a lot different than most types of fishing, in that you don't cast like a normal fishing pole. Instead, you strip out line, and use the rod bring all of the line into the air at the same time, back and behind you. Once you get the hang of it, it's a lot of fun.

Dark shadows lurked like silent monsters along the riverbank. Normally, it would be hard for most people to fly fish the AuSable after dark, but I knew the river like the back of my hand . . . even when it was late at night. I knew where the deep holes were, and where the sunken logs and rocks were. I knew where the trees hung out over the water, so I wouldn't get my fly caught on a limb. I knew where the big fish lurked, too.

And I love fishing the AuSable after dark, after most other fishermen have gone home. Night time on the AuSable River is when the big brown trout came out of the deep holes. They slither into shallower water, near the banks, in search of food. It's the best time to fish, but it's also the most challenging.

And, I make my own flies. The technique is called fly tying, and I make flies using a bare hook, thread, and animal fur and bird feathers. Oh, there are a lot of other things you can use, but mostly, flies are tied with natural fur and feathers.

Although it was too dark to see where my fly had landed, I heard the thin *plop!* as it landed on the water. I knew that it had landed right where I wanted it.

I let the current pull the line, and I gave the rod a few twitches. I was using a new fly pattern, one that I had made up on my own. I had never used this particular fly before, so I wasn't sure how well it would work. Some flies work better than others at different times.

Suddenly, the water exploded about thirty feet away, right where I knew my fly was! It was so sudden and unexpected that I almost jumped out of my waders! There was a sharp tug on my rod, and I held it tight, giving it a tug to set the hook.

The rod bent, and I knew that I had a fish on.

Boy . . . was I in for a surprise!

I was sure that I had hooked into a big brown trout. He was a real fighter, too, sweeping back and forth across the river, diving into a deep hole, and then heading downstream. Once, he leapt all the way out of the water. I caught only a glimpse of him in the darkness . . . but it was enough to tell me that something wasn't right. I couldn't put my finger on it, but I was sure of it.

Something wasn't quite right with this brown trout.

I battled for nearly ten minutes before the fish grew tired. In the darkness, I still couldn't see the fish. I pulled him closer and closer, holding my rod high with my right hand. My penlight was clipped to my vest, and I turned it on with my free hand. Then I readied the net.

Just a little bit closer . . . .

The fish splashed at the surface, then dove down again. I tried to scoop him up into my net, but I missed.

Carefully, I brought him close again. The fish was really fighting! I extended the net out a bit farther, waiting for him to get nearer so I wouldn't miss. After all, I didn't want to get him so close . . . only to have him break my line.

In the beam of my small penlight, I saw the fish. I seized the opportunity and plunged the net into the water.

Got him!

Although I couldn't see him, I could tell by the weight in the net that he wasn't going to get away, that the fish was securely in the net.

I pulled the net from the water, held it beneath the glowing light . . . and gasped at what I was holding.

The thing in my net wasn't a brown trout.

It wasn't a brook trout.

It was the biggest rainbow trout I had ever seen in the AuSable! Now, I know that might not seem like a big deal to *you,* but, where I live, there aren't very many rainbow trout. I only catch a couple of them a year, and I've never caught any big ones.

But this fish was beautiful! He was almost twenty inches long. He was covered with colorful spots. A bright pink and orange band ran along his side.

"Wow," I said out loud, marveling at my catch.

The fish made a sudden thrash in the net, splashing water all over.

"Hold on, buddy," I said, and I tucked my fly rod under my right arm to free up my hand. Then I dunked my hand into the water to get it wet. Before you handle a fish, it's a good idea to get your hand wet, so that your dry skin doesn't injure him.

I reached into the net and picked up the trout. He struggled and squirmed, but I was able to pull him out of the net without a problem.

I held the fish beneath my light, and again marveled at his size and color.

And on my new fly, too! One that I had created!

Cool beans.

Carefully, I unhooked the fly from the trout's mouth. It took a moment, because the fish kept struggling to get away. Once, my rod almost fell from under my arm.

After the trout was unhooked, I took one more long look at him. He sure was a beautiful fish, and I was really proud of myself.

Gently, I lowered him into the rustling river. As soon as his belly touched the water he gave a powerful thrash with his tail and vanished into the dark water, to live another day and perhaps be caught by another fisherman.

It was then that I noticed something.

The night had become deathly silent. The crickets had stopped chirping, and the frogs were no longer croaking. The only thing I could hear was the rippling river as it rushed around my waders in the waist-deep waters.

Strange.

I looked up into the night sky. The dark silhouettes of trees rose up like tribal lances, obscuring many of the stars. The trail of the milky way curled across the heavens.

But there were no sounds.

Except . . . .

An odd sound from downstream caught my attention. It was a repetitive, whooshing sound, and it was very faint.

But it quickly became louder.

Louder.

Louder, still . . . .

And it sounded like—

Like *wings*.

My tiny penlight was useless, because the beam only shone a few feet in front of me.

The sound grew louder, still.

But when I saw what was making the sound, I knew that it was already too late to get away.

The thing that was coming at me was huge! I caught a glimpse of giant wings, just above the water. It was terrible.

There was nothing else I could do but duck down into the water. I knew that I would get soaked, and water would fill my waders, but it would be a lot better than being carried away by that awful flying beast!

I bent over and fell into the water . . . just as the giant wings flapped over my head. The creature let out a terrible screech, and I knew that I probably scared it more than it had scared me.

In the next instant, the creature had passed. I was still in the water, and I turned to look upstream. It was then that I saw what it was.

A great blue heron, a very large bird that is pretty common on the AuSable, and a lot of other rivers and lakes in Michigan and other states. In fact, if you live near water in Michigan, there's a good chance you've seen a blue heron . . . so you know just how big they are.

I shook my head and laughed, struggling to stand up. Cold water had gushed into my waders, making them heavy and cumbersome.

"Great, Craig," I whispered. *"It'll be a cold walk home."*

Water dripped from my hat, my vest, and my arms. I was completely soaked. When I got home, I would have to take all of the things out of my vest so they could dry.

But it could have been worse. If the blue heron would have accidentally hit me, we both could have been in big trouble.

However, now I had something else to worry about.

The bird had come upon me so suddenly that I had dropped my fly into the water. The current had carried it downstream, where it was dangling in the middle of the river.

But that's not what the problem was.

The problem came when I began to reel it in.

That's when the water exploded, and my fly rod was nearly yanked out of my hand. I gave it a tug—more out of surprise than anything—and felt the hook take hold.

My rod bent so far that I thought it was going to break.

Up until that point, I had planned on going home. I was cold and wet, and it was getting late.

Now, however, I was going to battle yet another fish.

At least, that's what I thought. I had no reason to suspect that what had struck my fly wasn't a fish. I was sure that it was a big brown trout, or, maybe another rainbow.

I had no idea that what was on the other end of the line wasn't even a fish . . . nor did I realize the danger that was only moments away.

I quickly forgot about how cold and wet I was. I forgot about the great blue heron that had scared me.

The only thing I could think about was landing the fish at the end of my line.

But there was something strange about how the fish was fighting. It didn't feel like it was big—probably not as big as the rainbow trout I had caught—but the fish was very sluggish. Usually, a trout will dart and dive all over the place, trying to break the line and get away.

This fish, however, didn't do that. It was slow in its movements, and it had yet to come to the surface. The fish seemed to want to dive into a deep hole and lay there like a log.

I struggled to bring him in closer. I succeeded a few times, but, every time he drew near, he took off, and I had to let line out so that the fish wouldn't break it.

Wow, I thought. *Two big fish in one night! Wait until I tell Mom and Dad!*

Gradually, I was able to bring the fish closer. He had yet to surface, so I had no idea what kind he was . . . but I was sure he was a big ol' brown. He fought sluggishly, but I had no reason to think that what I was fighting would be anything but a fish.

Until I caught a glimpse of him in my penlight.

It was only a flash, for a quick moment.

But what I saw didn't look like the colors of a brown trout.

Or a rainbow trout.

It was too big to be a brook trout.

And was I mistaken . . . or did the fish look like it had . . . ridged *scales?*

It took another dive into deeper water, and I let out more line. But already, I could sense the fish getting tired. It wouldn't be long before I had him in my net.

Soon, the fish was almost within reach. I held the net in one hand, my fly rod in the other, slowly working the fish closer. He was still hidden in the dark, churning water, and I knew that, as soon as he surfaced, I would have to be quick.

Gently, I raised my fly rod higher, bringing the fish closer to the surface. In my other hand, I was ready with the net.

Suddenly, the creature appeared.

Immediately, I was gripped by shock and fear. Panic instantly set in as I gazed at what was on the line.

Dark, beady eyes glared at me. Razor-sharp teeth shined in the beam of my penlight. Dark, ruddy brown scales glistened.

I knew that what I was seeing couldn't be real.

It couldn't be true.

But it was.

Right here, in the AuSable River, at the end of my line with a fly hooked in it's mouth, was an alligator. He wasn't very big—maybe about the size of the rainbow trout I'd caught earlier—but that didn't mean that the creature wasn't dangerous.

I wanted to throw down my net, toss my rod into the water and run. I had to get away, out of the water. I had to get home. Mom and Dad would know what to do.

But before I could even react, the alligator opened its jaws even wider. It hissed loudly . . . and with a powerful swish of its tail, the beast lunged right at me.

About the author

Johnathan Rand is the author of the best-selling **'Chillers'** series, now with over 2,000,000 copies in print. In addition to the **'Chillers'** series, Rand is also the author of the **'Adventure Club'** series, including **'Ghost in the Graveyard'**, **'Ghost in the Grand'**, and **'The Haunted Schoolhouse'**, three collections of thrilling, original short stories. When Mr. Rand and his wife are not traveling to schools and book signings, they live in a small town in northern lower Michigan with their two dogs, Abby and Lily Munster. He is currently working on more 'Chillers', as well as a new series for younger readers entitled **'Freddie Fernortner, Fearless First Grader'**. His popular website features hundreds of photographs, stories, and art work. Visit:

www.americanchillers.com

Also by Johnathan Rand:

GHOST IN THE GRAVEYARD

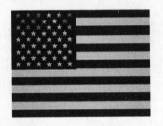